Her Forbidden Amish Love

Jocelyn McClay

LOVE INSPIRED

INSPIRATIONAL ROMANCE

Recycling programs for this product may not exist in your area.

ISBN-13: 978-1-335-48866-4

Her Forbidden Amish Love

This edition published by arrangement with Harlequin Books S.A.

For questions and comments about the quality of this book, please contact us at CustomerService@Harlequin.com.

Love Inspired
22 Adelaide St. West, 40th Floor
Toronto, Ontario M5H 4E3, Canada
www.Harlequin.com

Printed in U.S.A.

"I've missed you, Hannah."

Her eyes were wide. Liquid with tears behind the dark blue. "I…"

Gabe held his breath, waiting to hear why she'd abruptly abandoned him years before. Pressing her lips together, Hannah glanced away to stare out the window. Instantly, she stiffened.

"What is it?"

"Barb mentioned you were moved in?" Arms crossed tightly over her chest, Hannah was scanning the rest of the small, sparsely furnished apartment. "There's not much here."

At least her comment admitted that she had talked with her employer about him. It wasn't much, but he'd take it. "Well, I haven't collected much. There are some boxes yet to unpack in the kitchen. Some more still in my vehicle. Otherwise, that's about it. Did you think I was kidding when I said I needed curtains to cheer the place up?"

Her gaze was fixed on his well-worn brown couch. "I thought you had other motives."

It was the closest she'd come to mentioning their past. "I did."

Growing up on a farm, **Jocelyn McClay** enjoyed livestock and pursued a degree in agriculture. She met her husband while weight lifting in a small town—he "spotted" her. After thirty years in business management, they moved to an acreage in southeastern Missouri to be closer to family when their eldest of three daughters made them grandparents. When not writing, she keeps busy hiking, bike riding, gardening, knitting and substitute teaching.

Books by Jocelyn McClay

Love Inspired

The Amish Bachelor's Choice
Amish Reckoning
Her Forbidden Amish Love

Visit the Author Profile page at Harlequin.com.

Ask, and it shall be given you; seek, and ye shall find; knock, and it shall be opened unto you.
—*Matthew* 7:7

First and always,
thanks to God for this opportunity.

This book is dedicated to my mom, Barbara.
Thanks for exposing me to the joy of
exploring quilt shops. I'm so glad I have
projects that we found in them together.
You don't own a quilt shop in real life,
so here is one for you in this story.

Thanks to my uncle Gale, who lives within an
Amish community, for his insight.

Thanks to Misti and Joe, who began as terrific
resources of paramedic work and quickly
became wonderful friends.

Thank you to Saundra for answering my
quilt shop questions and having lovely
inventory to tempt me for future undertakings.

Thanks to Amy of the local animal shelter,
who took the time to advise on puppy care.

Any mistakes made on the above topics
are entirely my own.

Chapter One

It was Socks's soft yip that alerted her. Hannah Lapp looked up from snipping across the dark green material to see her expectant friend, Ruth Schrock, sway as she rose from her seat. Dropping the scissors, Hannah shot out a helpless hand as Ruth grabbed at the shelf behind her, bolts of fabric slowing her descent as she slid to the floor. Now the brightly hued material lay about Ruth's unmoving figure in a kaleidoscope of color.

"Is she having the baby?" Barbara Fastle, the *Englisch* owner of The Stitch quilt shop, asked as she and Rachel, an Amish customer, hurried from the back of the shop. "She seemed fine when she was sitting there a moment ago."

Hannah darted around the counter to kneel at Ruth's side. Tentatively touching her friend's face, she took in her closed eyes and pale color. "I don't think so. But I'm not sure." She carefully moved a nearly empty bolt that lay over Ruth's torso and placed a gentle hand on the woman's protruding stomach. When she felt an abrupt kick against her palm, but no tightening of flesh, Hannah exhaled in relief.

Looking up, her gaze connected with two hovering faces that shared her concern. It was obvious that Louisa Weaver's death a short month ago, along with her unborn child's, was foremost in their collective minds. Hannah's stomach clenched at the possibility of her friend meeting the same fate. "Rachel, run down to the furniture shop and get Malachi. He needs to be here." An instant later, the bell over the door jangled frantically as the young Amish woman dashed out.

"That EMT guy—" hastening toward the counter and the portable phone, Barb waggled her hand urgently as if it would assist her in what she was trying to say "—the one they had the grant for. He rented the apartment upstairs. Moved in this weekend. He'd be the fastest help. Run up and see if he's there. If not, I'll call 911 and get something rolling from out of town, but it'll be a while before they can get here."

Jumping to her feet, Hannah rushed toward the rear of the store where an exit opened into a short hallway, her dog Socks at her heels. Bursting through the brightly painted door, Hannah pivoted from the alley entrance and toward the interior stairway that led up to the small apartment the elderly shop owner occasionally rented out. Hannah's heart was racing faster than her black-soled shoes as she pounded up the steps' worn linoleum.

Hammering rapidly on the paneled wooden door, Hannah shot a worried look back down the narrow stairway as if she could still see her friend lying among the fallen bolts of fabric. Spying a concerned Socks on the steps, Hannah pointed for the Border collie to retreat to the bottom. When the door clicked open, she whipped her head back.

At the sight of the man in the open doorway, Hannah gasped and her eyes widened. Mind whirling, she stepped back into the empty space of the stairwell. Only the hand that shot out to close around her wrist kept Hannah from tumbling down to land in a heap at the base of the stairs. She found herself pulled against a broad chest as strong arms wrapped about her back. The sensation was as riotous as the fall down the stairs would've been. Socks's anxious bark barely penetrated the buzzing in her ears.

Her nose was tucked under a smooth-shaven jaw. If anything, her heart rate accelerated at the sensation. She knew that jawline. If her sister hadn't left that day, it would've been the one Hannah gazed at across the breakfast table for the past five years.

But Gail had walked away.

And Hannah had made the difficult decision to cut Gabriel Bartel out of her life.

Her fingers throbbing against the sturdy chest that cushioned her, Hannah inhaled the scent of male and fresh soap before gingerly pushing away, careful this time to stay on the small landing. Gabriel's hands slid from her back and down the sleeves of her dress to lightly encircle her wrists. Tapping with her toe into the area behind her until she felt the first step, Hannah hastily stepped onto it. Their arms stretched out between them before he opened his hands and released her. From the base of the stairs, Socks's barks receded to a few concerned woofs.

"I need…" Hannah swallowed, firmly pushed her shock aside and started again. "*We* need your help downstairs. Ruth has—a woman has fainted, a woman who's with child…" The blood drained from Hannah's face when Gabe stepped back into the apartment, leaving her standing on the step. Surely he wouldn't refuse to help because of their past? She puffed out a breath in relief when he reappeared a moment later, carrying a small pack.

"My jump bag. Contains a few necessary pieces of equipment. Let's go." He gestured for Hannah to lead them down the narrow steps.

She fled down them as if the turbulent waters of a broken dam were lashing at her heels. What followed her down was even more frightening. Memories of her past, suppressed these past years, now unleashed churning emotions—shock, excitement, longing, regret. If it wasn't for her fear for Ruth, Hannah might've taken the exit to the alley, hastily hitched up her buggy horse, Daisy, and headed home to lick wounds—long-thought healed—that now throbbed anew.

Instead, she burst through the back door into the quilt shop, Socks at her heels, to find Ruth still slumped on the floor with Barbara, her brow creased in deep lines, crouched beside her. The shop owner stood and backed away, relief apparent on her face as Gabe hastened forward.

"She hasn't moved."

Gabe nodded as he took her place beside the unconscious woman. Sliding Ruth's black cloak aside, he picked up her limp wrist, resting his fingers on the blue-veined skin. "Her pulse is slow, but steady. Did she hit her head in the fall?" When Barb and Hannah promptly shook their heads, he untied and gently loosened the black bonnet.

Ruth's arms and legs shifted. Conscious of keeping

out of the way, Hannah crouched down close enough to see her friend's eyes flutter. Hannah opened her mouth to talk to Ruth, before glancing at Gabe to see if she should do so. Apparently interpreting her look, he nodded as he continued his examination.

"Ruth! Are you all right?"

"Just got a little dizzy when I stood up." Eyes fully open now, Ruth looked confused at finding herself on the floor amid the bolts of fabric. She leaned forward, attempting to stand.

"Let's not be in any hurry to get up." Gabe moved into her line of sight, a reassuring smile on his face. Hannah swallowed, trying not to remember when his smiles had been directed at her. When his comforting baritone could make her believe that everything would be all right for them, too. "You've had a fall. Let's make sure you and your little passenger are ready before we stand. Just think of it as a moment to examine some of this lovely material more closely, okay?"

Ruth's eyes rounded and her arms swept protectively around her stomach. "My *boppeli*!"

"Seems like he's doing okay and not interested in making his first appearance in a quilt shop," Gabe responded immediately, his voice soothing. "Does your head, neck or back hurt? No? Then let's get you on to your side and give you two another moment before we go further." He assisted Ruth in shifting her position, cushioning her protruding stomach with a bolt of dark blue fabric. "Do you get dizzy often?"

"*Nee*. Only when I…" Ruth stopped and frowned.

"Only when you…?" Gabe slipped a blood pressure cuff on her arm.

"Only when I forget to eat." The admission seemed dragged from the prone woman.

"Ah, that does make a difference." With a glance at the reading, he slipped the cuff off. "What is it that they say? You're eating for two? Me, I'm starved by this time of day just eating for one." He sat back on his heels. "You want to try sitting up?"

Hannah, still rooted where she knelt by Ruth, couldn't tear her eyes from Gabe's confident, fluid movements. The light brown curly hair and deep green eyes were the same, but this wasn't the youth she'd met and quickly fallen for at a party almost five years earlier. That'd been a charming boy. This was a capable man. And she was sure she'd memorized every detail about him then, down to the crease in his lean cheeks when he smiled, but she couldn't recall him ever mentioning an interest in medical care.

"Ja." Ruth's mutter, her voice tinged with self-disgust drew Hannah's attention.

Gabe smiled gently. "Your vitals are fine. Probably low blood sugar. I can't recommend missing meals in your state." Following a pointed look from him that scattered her breathing until she understood his intent, Hannah helped Gabe settle Ruth into the chair her friend had been sitting on ten minutes earlier. Once settled, Ruth wrapped her hands around her stomach again and looked fully into Gabe's attentive face.

Her brows furrowed. "I remember you."

Hannah opened her mouth to say something—offer to run for cookies or juice, or promise to make another quilt for the baby—anything to change the imminent subject. She didn't want Ruth's sharp mind to place where she'd previously seen the man now tending her.

Ruth had been with her at the first party, but any further meetings Hannah had had with Gabe—and there'd been several—had been private. Treasured. Innocent. And too precious to share even with her closest friend.

To her relief, before Hannah could say a word, bells jangled wildly as the shop's front door burst open and Ruth's husband, pale-faced and coatless, rushed in. Rachel Mast, a few steps behind, shut the door against the January cold. Dodging through the rows of multihued fabric, Malachi Schrock was kneeling at his wife's side a moment later.

Along with the blast of winter air, a tension pervaded the shop. Now that Ruth was alert and seemingly recovered, Hannah felt the weight of Gabe's gaze. Knotting her fingers together, she tried to ignore its compelling lure. Her heart raced as if she was still running up the stairs. She expelled her breath in a rush when Barbara spoke. "Good thing you're here, Malachi. Ruth is remembering strange men."

Hannah's eyes finally met Gabe's. He wasn't a stranger. He was the man she'd loved. The man she'd been going to build a life with. Until she'd been reminded her community was more important. A community whose leaders were now mentioning more and more often that it was past time Hannah Lapp be baptized and marry one of its men. Dropping her gaze, she knelt to slide her fingers into Socks's soft, comforting fur. Hannah knew she should, and would, do as they willed, even though it would be without love for the man. Because she'd only ever loved once. And the Mennonite man standing before her was definitely not an acceptable option for her to marry.

* * *

She wasn't going to acknowledge him. Dropping his gaze, Gabe watched the man entwine his work-roughened fingers with his wife's. Gabe returned his attention to Hannah, longing to do the same. Her slender hands were tangled in the dog's black fur. Just like years ago, she'd withdrawn.

But this time, unlike years ago, he wasn't going to let her avoid him and disappear.

The married couple held a brief, private discussion, while Gabe ran an assessing eye over his temporary patient. He didn't ask when the baby was due. Amish women weren't fixated on their due dates like *Englisch* women were, figuring babies would arrive when they were ready. After checking with Gabe that it was all right to move her, Malachi Schrock gathered his auburn-haired wife protectively under his arm and they exited the shop. Their voices trailed behind them as he shouldered the door open to let in a stream of cold air along with a few whirling snowflakes. The wood-and-glass door shut with a rattle. When the accompanying clatter of the bell faded away, the remaining four in the shop glanced at each other in the silence.

Correction, Hannah glanced at Gabe before her gaze skittered away again. She immediately straightened and busied herself, picking up the fallen bolts of fabric. The Border collie at her side evaluated Gabe through intelligent brown eyes before trotting to a dog bed tucked along the wall. He watched her rest her muzzle on her white legs as she continued to study him.

Well, at least he had the attention of one of them. *You're here now, Bartel. Begin as you mean to go on.* This time, he wasn't going to let Hannah avoid him.

Picking up a bolt of dark blue material, he handed it to her. Eyes he knew were almost a matching shade remained carefully averted as Hannah hesitated before accepting the fabric. Gabe picked up another bolt, this time shifting it in his hands to ensure his fingers touched Hannah's when she tentatively reached for it. Flinching at the contact, she darted a look at him as the heavy bolt sagged between them. Gabe met Hannah's wary look with a bland smile. *You're not going to ignore me.* She must've gotten the hint, as she hefted the fabric onto the shelf, turning her back to him as she did so.

The gray-haired shop owner had stepped behind a wide counter and picked up the orange-handled scissors lying on dark green material spread out upon it. "Well, that was exciting. I thought we might have to pull down the baby quilts and put them to use. I hope Ruth is all right. Rachel, was there anything else you needed?"

Gabe didn't recognize the young woman who'd entered with Ruth's husband. She looked younger than Hannah, so she might not have been in her *rumspringa* at the same time as the slender woman whose blue eyes continued to avoid his as she smoothed out the bolts, which were now lining the shelf again.

He'd recognized Ruth, though. She'd been there when he'd first met Hannah. And had looked on doubtfully as he'd introduced himself and clumsily tried to charm her beautiful, reserved friend.

Fortunately for him, something he'd said that night had worked. Either that, or Hannah had taken pity on him, because she'd agreed to meet with him again. And again. And many times over during the wonderful beginning of that summer. Until the night Gabe had paced

the ground of their prearranged location, anxiously re-
hearsing a marriage proposal. And she'd never shown.

He hadn't seen her since.

But he hadn't forgotten her. And he'd always kept
his ear to the ground in regard to Miller's Creek.

When this job opportunity arose at the same time
he'd heard rumors that Hannah would be taking baptism
classes so she could marry, it was like God was giving
him a nudge. Gabe knew that once Hannah became a
baptized member of the church, she'd never marry a
Mennonite like himself and be shunned from her family and community. He'd been given a second chance.

He was going to make the most of it.

Frowning, Gabe repacked his jump bag as he regarded the precisely pleated back of the *kapp* covering
Hannah's neatly pinned golden blond hair. As he retraced his steps to the back of the shop at a much slower
pace than when he'd entered, his new landlady looked
up from cutting fabric and called out to thank him. His
glance at Hannah was rewarded only with a brief, cool
nod before she studiously continued her task.

Her composed profile was the last thing Gabe
saw before he ducked through the cheerful rear door.
Climbing the steps to his apartment, he snorted wryly.
What had he been expecting? That she'd just fall into
his arms once she saw him again? Gabe's lips twisted
as he recalled she'd done just that, for a moment. But
whatever had prevented her from meeting him that
night still had her shutting him out. Well, he faced
challenges every day in his job. He wasn't one to shy
away from a tough situation. Gabe knew convincing
Hannah to marry him would be that and more.

Chapter Two

Hannah was glad to be out of The Stitch for even the few minutes it took to walk to the post office and retrieve the shop's mail. At least these were moments when her ears weren't tuned to the bang of the shop's back door. After two days, she could finally resist whipping her head toward the door at any sound generated behind it, as it might announce Gabriel Bartel's appearance. It was surely understandable to be jumpy regarding Gabe's actions. The man had just popped unexpectedly back into her life. It certainly wasn't eagerness to see him that had her looking in that direction at the sound of his feet on the stairs. Or so she told herself.

Ruth, thankfully, seemed to have recovered from the incident. Hannah didn't know if she ever would. The night she'd forced herself to stay home from meeting with Gabe had been one of the hardest things she'd ever done. Second only to watching her pregnant sister, Gail, walk away from home and the Amish community earlier that day.

If Gail hadn't left, Hannah might've made a differ-

ent choice. But seeing what her departure had done
to her family had made Hannah ill. The heartache of
her parents. The whispering of those that gossiped.
The pitying looks of those that didn't. The suspicious
eyes on her and her younger brothers, wondering if
they too might abandon the Amish lifestyle. Hannah,
who'd always abided by *gelassenheit*, obeying the will
of those in authority, had felt the heavy weight of their
stares and disapproval.

She'd vowed, in the lonely bedroom she'd shared
with her sister, to never disappoint her parents. And
so her dreams for a life with the Mennonite man she
loved had disappeared down the road with Gail.

Hannah jumped at the harsh scrape of metal on
concrete behind her. Spinning around, she and Socks,
who'd been trotting on a leash at her side, watched as
a man hastily exited the car that'd just slid its rusted
nose onto the high sidewalk. Hannah backed away as
the man lunged up the steep step and stood swaying
before her. She flinched again at Socks's unexpected
soft growl.

The man's stringy hair blew over his face. He made
an attempt to straighten his jacket, a futile action, as
the coat was buttoned crooked. Something had con-
gealed into dark patches on his worn blue jeans. A
sliver of unease rippled up Hannah's spine. She slid
another step back as Socks brushed against her leg.

"Nice dog." The man's voice was low and rough,
like scraping a shovel over a bed of rocks. There was
something in it that made the comment sound not like
a compliment, but a threat. Giving a faint nod, Han-

nah slipped her hand through the end of Socks's leash and tightened her grip on the leather.

"Border collie, right? They're good working dogs. Does she bite?"

Hannah huffed out a tight breath when another car pulled up to the sidewalk, briefly drawing the man's attention. "I…I need to get back to work." Pivoting, she doubled her speed, willing to take her chances of sliding over the snow-frosted surface. Several steps farther, she risked a glance back. The man was watching them. Hannah was used to *Englisch* visitors to town staring at times, curious about Amish dress and lifestyle. But this one wasn't looking at her. His attention was on Socks.

Hannah was breathless when she and Socks swept into the shop and closed the heavy door behind them. A condition that wasn't helped when she looked over the tops of the myriad bolts of fabric to see the curly-haired man talking with her employer. Striving to collect herself, she leaned down and unsnapped Socks's leash.

Upon straightening, she almost headed out the door again at Barb's words. "We were just talking about you."

"Oh, really?" Chagrined to hear her voice an octave higher than normal, Hannah cleared her throat and tried again as she hung up her cloak on the wall peg by the door. "How so?"

"Gabe was asking if we made the quilts." The older woman gestured to the collection of intricately designed blankets that lined the walls of the shop. "I was telling him I make some, but you're the more talented one." Barb turned back to Gabe who, one muscular shoulder leaning against the wall, was watching Hannah as she threaded her way through the maze of fabric.

After facing the unsettling man on the sidewalk, Hannah blinked her eyes at the surge of temptation to tuck against Gabe's side. Feel his arm slide over her shoulder. Relax in the remembered comfort of being close to his solid form. Stumbling, she reached out to put a hand on the smooth cotton of a bolt beside her, steadying herself. She could not fall again for this man. He was not for her. She should've forgotten him years ago. Pressing her lips together, Hannah stiffened her resolve and her knees along with it.

His eyes never leaving her face, Gabe tilted one corner of his mouth into a crooked smile and straightened from his slouch against the wall when she reached them.

"Who made the rest of them?"

To Hannah's relief, Barb fielded his question. "Some of the Amish ladies in the community bring their projects in, and we sell them on commission. I'd love to carry more, but they're busy women."

"I can imagine." He winced, frowning in consideration. "That might make my request unfeasible."

"Much is lost for want of asking." Barb repinned some loose fabric back onto a bolt on the counter and returned it to the shelf.

"I was wondering if it would be possible to get some curtains for the windows upstairs that face the street. I never know when I might be called out and I don't want to disturb neighbors when my lights come on in the middle of the night." He shrugged. "I suppose I could stop at the big box store in Portage my next time through and buy some premade ones, but I noticed some of your...art." He glanced around him at the displays. "There's really no other word for it. I thought something like that might be cheery, as well as functional upstairs."

"It is pretty dreary up there, isn't it? I should've thought of that. I haven't rented it out since the young Hershberger couple lived there for some months after they were married, waiting for their house to be built." The gray-haired woman grinned. "With Ophelia the oldest of thirteen children, there wasn't room for them to stay with her folks other than the traditional night after their wedding."

Hannah frowned. Freeman and Ophelia Hershberger already had a two-year-old son and another one on the way. Why hadn't Barb rented out the apartment since then? Why now? It would've been considerably easier on Hannah's peace of mind to have another young Amish couple banging their way through the back door to the alley instead of the current tenant.

The shop owner leaned an elbow on a row of various shades of blue fabric. "Which reminds me of something else. Besides curtains, do you have everything you need? The apartment has electricity, but it hasn't been used by an *Englisch* person for some time."

Hannah sucked in a quiet breath at Gabe's grin. The sight of it still made her stomach jump like a summer night full of fireflies.

"I did find that I'm well supplied with oil lamps in case the power goes out. And the additional heat source is nice. And I'm Mennonite. As were the Amish originally. There was a falling out sometime in the 17th century and we're a bit more comfortable with technology, but there are still similarities to the Amish. Some of us even speak the same language. At least we used to. *Ja?*"

Hannah's cheeks heated when Gabe turned to her with a raised eyebrow. She knew he was referring to their earlier time together, not Pennsylvania Dutch, the dialect Amish and some Mennonite spoke. She and Gabe used to want the same thing—to live their lives together. Hannah wasn't sure what he wanted now, dropping back into her life. But what she wanted had changed. It had to have. She wanted to stay in her community. To not cause ripples. To submit to the will of the *Diener*—the district's elected officials—and not distress her parents. Still, her mouth grew dry and the flush crept down her neck under Gabe's intent regard.

"Well, we're glad the grant went through to establish an EMS program in town. But there are probably better places in the area to rent." Barb wagged a finger toward the ceiling and the living space above it. "Whatever prompted you to want my little apartment upstairs?"

"Oh, the price was right. And I liked the location." Gabe smiled at her employer, but his tone and the glance he returned to Hannah were deceptively neutral. Still, Hannah figured her cheeks were now the hue of the brightest red fabric in the shop. Peering at the door, she willed a customer to walk in. To her dismay, their side of the snow-covered street was empty.

She focused her attention on Barb, only to find her employer looking between her and Gabe speculatively.

The older woman straightened away from the bolts of fabric. "So you need curtains. You're right. You're living above a quilt shop. We can't let you put store-bought curtains up there. Hannah can make them for you."

Hannah's jaw dropped. She barely managed to squeak, "Me? Amish don't generally have curtains."

"*Englisch* customers love to see you working on the treadle sewing machine when they come in. Helps make the shop seem quaint. Besides, you're a better seamstress than I am. If you can figure pattern calculations for quilting, you can figure out curtains. I can handle other things while you work on them."

"But…"

Ignoring her, Barb turned to Gabe and waved her hand at the surrounding shop. "What color did you have in mind?"

His attention on Hannah's rounded eyes, Gabe offered, "I'm partial to blue."

The shop owner patted the fabric beside her. "We can certainly do that. Anything here you like?"

Gabe's eyes remained locked with Hannah's. "Yes," he drawled.

She looked away. He was flustering her, charming her, all over again. She couldn't let it happen.

Striding over to the row of blue fabrics, she smacked the bolted material. "Pick one." Forcing a smile, Hannah released a breath. Her smile faded as she recalled how close she'd come to disrupting her world for this man. Crossing her arms over her chest, Hannah reminded herself Gabe was as out of place in her life as his muscular and masculine form was in the bright-colored quilt shop that surrounded him.

Although she stood her ground, her heart rate escalated as Gabe strolled closer to survey the vast collection of fabrics, some plain in keeping with Amish needs, some with printed design to accommodate *Englisch* shoppers. All in shades of blue from the lightest pastel to the deepest navy. "Hmm. That's a tough one." He glanced over at Hannah, standing stiffly at the end of the row.

"Well, it'd be nice to wake up to something beautiful. Although beauty isn't everything. It's more how it makes you feel." Reaching out a hand, he traced a finger down the length of a nearby bolt. Hannah forced her attention away from it. "I'd like something that seems cool at the outset." Gabe paused as his eyes slid to the fabric before returning to her rigid form. "But vibrant upon closer scrutiny."

Pressing her lips together, Hannah glanced over to see Barb watching with raised eyebrows. She wanted to put her hand over Gabe's mouth to keep him from continuing. But the thought of touching him reminded her of the warm skin of his cheek, and the soft bristle that grew there when they would meet late in the day. Hannah curled her hands into fists to dismiss the sensation. Her short nails dug into her palms as he continued.

"I want something that makes me feel alive as I start the day, but is restful at the end of it." Gabe squinted thoughtfully as he deliberated. "Something that's more complicated than it actually seems. Something that has a bit of glow to it."

At each description, Gabe's gaze shifted from the fabric to her face. Hannah fixed her gaze away from him and blew out another breath, determined not to let him fluster her further. She remembered how he'd always made her laugh. She'd never laughed so much as when they'd been together. Hannah frowned. She'd missed that. It was almost as if the colors of her life were somehow muted now that Gabe was no longer in it.

She narrowed her eyes at the row of material she faced. Beige. A neutral color, normally a background in the concept of the quilt. That was her. She wasn't a vibrant blue. Gabe was describing someone Hannah didn't recognize. One who didn't exist anymore. Or maybe only had with him. Hannah swallowed. And she wasn't just beige. She was beige without a pattern in the fabric, like the *Englisch* preferred. Bland. Muted.

Only Gabe had made her feel like the primary focus of a design.

Hannah's eyes burned. She blinked until the fabric went from a blur back to individual shades of pale, sandy, yellowish-brown.

Biting the inside of her cheek, Hannah reminded herself that background colors were always needed. She'd heard murmurings from the district's *Diener*. According to those ministers, she'd soon be bound into some arrangement with another for life. Just not one of her choosing. With a slight turn of her head, Hannah met Gabe's green eyes. No, she'd given up her chance for creating her own design.

And it was past time Gabe finished this and choose

his. Whirling to face the blue fabrics, Hannah jerked a bolt out of the row.

"No, not that one. The one next to it," Gabe directed.

Hannah stuffed the one she had back and pulled the one he'd indicated. Striding over to the counter, she dropped it with a thud next to Barb.

"Nice shade," Barb commented as she eyed the bolt before sliding it over to the side. "It matches Hannah's eyes. But before I cut it, I need to know the required length. Hannah, you'll have to go up and measure the windows for him." The shop owner returned her attention to Gabe. "I'm assuming you know what style you want?"

"Plain," he responded immediately, his eyes dancing. "I like a plain style."

Hannah stifled a snort, her face flaming again. He'd keep this up until the silly curtains were made and hung. Her best recourse was to avoid him and be coolly pleasant when he was around. No one needed to know they had a history. And she couldn't allow them to have a future. Snagging the tape measure from the counter, Hannah strove for a composed stroll toward the back door. The sooner the measurements were taken, the sooner she could finish the project. These would be the fastest curtains ever made. And then she could go back to being beige. Where she'd been content these past few years.

Hadn't she?

Watching Hannah march to the store's rear exit, Gabe couldn't suppress the grin that spread across his face. He pulled out his billfold.

Barb waved it away. "Don't know what the cost is until we know how much material you're getting. Besides, I'll provide these with the apartment."

He repocketed the billfold. "When we know, I'll pay. I have a feeling I might take them with me no matter where I go." They both looked over when the back door slammed behind Hannah.

Barb narrowed her eyes at Gabe. "Where did you say you two had met?"

Gabe headed for the rear exit when he heard Hannah's determined tread on the stairs. "I didn't," he tossed back over his shoulder.

Since the door to the apartment wasn't locked, Hannah was already inside and at the window with her tape measure by the time Gabe stepped through the door. He wasn't surprised she had went straight to the task. From her behavior since he'd arrived, he figured it was so she could leave immediately, continuing to avoid him as much as possible.

She wasn't fooling him. Hannah was as aware of him as he was of her. Although she didn't turn when the door clicked closed, under the dark green fabric of her dress he saw her shoulder give a barely discernible flinch at the sound.

Gabe sighed. He paused, then reached back to open the door again. Maybe that'd been part of the problem before. The wonderful times they'd had together, the joy they'd felt with each other, the relationship they'd built—innocent except for their growing feelings—it hadn't been in the open.

If he was going to convince her to marry him, he'd have to drag it there.

Hannah rose on tiptoe, a lovely slender silhouette in front of the window, the weak winter light shining in around her. She stretched out her arm toward the top of the frame. Her reach was about four inches short of the wooden trim on the tall window.

"Here, let me help." Gabe's feet echoed on the bare wood floor as he hustled over to where she stood.

"I think you've helped enough," Hannah responded as she let the end of the tape measure dangle, leaving ample room for him to grab it without touching her fingers.

Gabe took the metal end tab and held it up above their heads. The stiff organza of her *kapp* was right under his chin. Her golden-blond hair was within kissing distance. Gabe was sorely tempted to drop a tender caress upon it as he'd done years before. Appreciated then, that action now would probably send Hannah skittering down the stairs. Frowning, he considered the scarred wooden trim of the window. "Where do you want it measured from?"

When Hannah looked up to assess, their eyes met and held for a moment before she slid hers away to peer at small holes in the wall just outside the trim. "Are those nail holes? They're probably from brackets for previous shades or curtain rods. Measure from there."

He moved the tape as she requested, trying to focus on the street below him instead of the citrus-shampoo scent of her hair. Only when she bent to measure the bottom of the window was he able to draw a full breath. "Funny how holes are left when something is no longer there that used to be."

She'd certainly left holes in him. Some he'd managed to plaster over through the years. Some that might never be filled again. Especially if he couldn't breach whatever barrier she'd put between them.

Hannah spoke to the sill below him. "Maybe it never should've been there in the first place."

Dropping his arm, he released the tape. "You don't believe that." He watched as she straightened, rolling the white length into a tight coil. "I've missed you, Hannah."

Her eyes were wide, liquid with tears. "I…"

Gabe held his breath, waiting to hear why she'd abruptly abandoned him years before. Pressing her lips together, Hannah glanced away to stare out the window. Instantly, she stiffened.

"What is it?" Gabe looked out the window when Hannah backed to the center of the room. Nothing seemed out of the ordinary on the street below. Shallow piles of snow edged the street. A scattering of cars were passing by. A handful of people were on the sidewalk, including a man directly below them.

"Barb mentioned you were all moved in." Arms crossed tightly over her chest, Hannah was scanning the rest of the small, sparsely furnished apartment. "There's not much here."

At least her comment admitted that she had talked with her employer about him. It wasn't much, but he'd take it. His breath escaped in a slow hiss at her obvious avoidance of their history as Gabe followed her gaze. "Well, I haven't collected much. There are some boxes yet to unpack in the kitchen. Some more still in my vehicle. Otherwise, that's about it. Did you think

I was kidding when I said I needed curtains to cheer the place up?"

Her gaze was fixed on his well-worn brown couch. "I thought you had other motives."

It was the closest she'd come to mentioning their past. "I did." Gabe studied her face. There were signs of strain under the polite composure. He longed to press her, but recognized the need to pursue a light present instead of bringing up their fractured past. "But it still was pretty dreary up here. I don't suppose you could make me a pillow for the couch, as well?"

"You'll be lucky to get the curtains," she retorted, but her lips curved in the first genuine smile he'd encountered since he'd seen her again. Ah, this was the Hannah he remembered.

"Well. What was it Barb had said? 'Much is lost for want of asking.'" He trailed after her to the apartment door. "Don't forget the window in the bedroom. It's the same size. Basically." He wobbled a hand in a so-so movement. "As far as old buildings go, anyway. I truly don't want to be a sideshow for anyone when I'm home. Or bother anyone else who happens to live downtown when I respond to a call at odd hours."

Hannah paused in the open doorway. "The community was thrilled when the grant went through to start the EMS service. How did you end up being the one…?"

"I saw the job opening and I was looking." *For a way to get into the area* remained unsaid. As did any mention of the solid-paying job he'd left to come here in exchange for the baseline salary the grant provided and a collection of part-time work that barely scraped up enough for the apartment and other living expenses. But if he could convince Hannah they belonged together, that and the difference he knew he could make in emergency care for the rural area would be enough reward.

"Will you be driving an ambulance and such?"

"I'll be going out on local calls, but there's a bit of groundwork to set up at first, like working with the newly identified medical director. The grant budget won't stretch to an ambulance." It barely paid for him to do local EMS work while he helped establish the program. "A share of the schedule will still be covered with volunteers. Part of the work I'll be doing is local fire department and EMS training, so folks like the Amish volunteers don't have to travel so far for it. Also, I'll be teaching CPR classes at the Portage hospital, as well as businesses and the junior college."

Hannah's brows furrowed. Gabe figured it was the mention of the college. He'd been studying something else years ago when, on a whim, he'd joined some friends at a weekend party that'd involved a mixture of local youth, including the woman before him.

The muffled jangle of the shop door drifted up the stairs. With a slight frown, Hannah turned her head in that direction. "I have to go. Barb might need some help downstairs."

Gabe winked at her. "Remember the measurements?"

Hannah's face went blank, and her blue eyes blinked a few rapid times before she recited the width and length of the window with a grin. "You were trying to distract me."

Gabe's own smile ebbed. "It's the other way around, Hannah. I've been distracted since I met you. You know why I really came to Miller's Creek."

The flawless skin of Hannah's cheeks bloomed in color. She fled down the worn linoleum steps of the narrow stairway. Gabe watched her descent. Had he made progress? It was hard to tell. But at least, for this moment, he knew why she was running away. And where he could find her again.

Hannah's heart was pounding as she raced down the stairs. She'd forgotten the joy of just being with Gabe. Maybe they could figure out some way of spending time together? Surely no harm could come of a few casual meetings? The possibility brought a smile to her face as she hustled along the short hallway. Her breathless grin abruptly faded as she stepped into the shop and pulled the back door closed. Facing the occupants in the shop who looked over at her entrance, she shuttered her mind to the thrill and temptation of being with Gabe.

Here was her life. Here was where her mind and obedience needed to be focused. Clasping her hands at her waist, she nodded to Barb to indicate she'd take care of these particular customers and propped up a composed smile to replace the earlier genuine one. Stepping away from the door, she greeted the two who'd arrived while she'd been upstairs. Enjoying herself, Hannah pushed the errant thought away.

"Ruby Weaver, Bishop Weaver, what a pleasure to see you both today. Is there anything I can help you with?" The statement was a stretch. The pleasure would be if they were truly here for material. And not to see her for some reason.

Any hope of that quickly died at the bishop's next words.

"Hannah Lapp. I need to talk with you." Bishop Weaver motioned Hannah over to the corner of racks displaying different quilting tools and patterns, away from where the *Englisch* store owner was working.

Hannah tried not to drag her feet. But she remembered all too well that Bishop Weaver and his wife were the reasons her *schweschder*, Gail, almost didn't return to Miller's Creek with her young daughter Lily. It was only thanks to *Gott* and the persistence of Samuel Schrock, now Gail's husband, that they'd rejoined the Amish community some months ago.

Shortly after Gail and Samuel's wedding, the bishop's only daughter-in-law and her unborn child had unexpectedly died. Bishop Weaver had pulled Hannah aside at Louisa's funeral and admonished her that it was time for her to take baptism classes and thereby become a member of the church.

As a member, she was eligible to marry.

Dread pooled in her stomach like water running into a dry creek bed following a hard rain. She knew what he was going to say. She knew what she was going to have to say in return as an Amish woman for whom *gelassenheit* was a way of life. Hannah swallowed hard to keep the hint of tears from glistening.

"Hannah Lapp. It is selfish of you to remain single at your age when our unmarried men need wives."

At twenty-three, Hannah was older than many single Amish women. It wasn't what she'd planned when she'd started her *rumspringa*. But then she'd met Gabriel. Even though she'd intentionally dropped out of his life, she hadn't been able to erase him from her mind. She'd since had many admirers, but no other young man in the Amish community had been tempting enough for Hannah to want to share their lives. Not in the way she'd wanted to share Gabe's. So she'd delayed. And delayed.

"You will marry one of our men shortly after your baptism. You might as well see who will suit." The bishop droned on, expecting her full attention and cooperation. Hannah bowed her head. *And why shouldn't he be? You've always done what was expected of you.*

Hannah braced herself. She knew who he was going to mention. It wasn't that she had anything against the man. He was hardworking and honorable. It was just that, in the times she'd been around him at different functions and church events, there was no spark. Nothing like she'd shared with…Gabe.

But that was years ago, when the man had been single. Hannah admonished herself to be open-minded. Perhaps things had changed since then. There were other Amish marriages that'd started out with not much more than friendship and respect and had grown into solid relationships. She could live with that. She'd just hoped for…something more.

"There is a man, recently widowed, in the community. I will tell him that you expect him to come calling. Plan for Jethro to be here tomorrow to take you to lunch."

And there it was. Bishop Weaver might state that she should start seeing the single men to see with whom she might suit, but what he'd meant was she was to marry his widowed son. His only son. Hannah felt the burn of distress in the back of her throat at the same time she stifled an inappropriate snort at the possibility that Jethro might have plans for the morrow, and his life, that his father wasn't aware of. Or more likely, didn't care about.

"*Denki*, Bishop Weaver. I will expect to see Jethro tomorrow. I appreciate your consideration and concern for my welfare." Hannah didn't know how she got the words out. They must have risen from the deep reservoir of practiced obedience she'd lived all her life, except for the brief, stolen time with Gabe years ago.

She'd always done the right thing. Been the well-behaved daughter to her sister Gail's more rebellious actions. Always thought of others first and herself later, if at all. Years of that behavior enabled her to respond appropriately to the bishop. But inside, her heart was breaking. *Oh, Gabe!* Hannah gently set her teeth together to keep her chin from trembling.

Bishop Weaver nodded jerkily before flinching. He raised a hand to rub it along his jaw and down his neck. Furrowing her brow at his actions, Hannah pushed aside her distress when she noted, even in the shop's temperate environment, beads of sweat were dotting his forehead under the brim of his hat.

"Are you all right?"

"*Ja,*" he mumbled, but his response was more distracted than his usual brusqueness. "Ruby," he called across the shop in a strained voice. "It's time to go."

Ruby's narrow face reflected her surprise at the abrupt directive. Hannah supposed it didn't happen very often. Probably, much more frequently, the other way around. But, with a glance at Hannah and Barb, she turned toward the front exit, her mouth pressed in a lipless line. Hand against his stomach, Bishop Weaver struggled to open the front door of the shop, the bell jangling with his repeated attempts. Finally he succeeded and shuffled out with hunched shoulders, his wife at his heels.

Hannah and Barb watched them climb into a nearby buggy, the bishop pausing on the step before he pulled himself in. "He didn't look like he felt well," Barb observed, frowning as her fingers automatically resumed the task of stocking a recent delivery of fat quarters— precut pieces of fabric popular among quilters.

Neither did Hannah after their conversation. The bishop's health was forgotten as she went to the counter, found a pad of paper and jotted down the measurements of the window upstairs. She was surprised she remembered them after her talk with the bishop. But then, she'd always remembered every moment of her interactions with Gabriel Bartel. Much as she'd once hoped differently, she knew now it was all she'd ever have of him.

Chapter Three

Hannah had always liked the cheery jingle of The Stitch's doorbell, knowing it announced a customer or someone just dropping by to visit. Today, she flinched at the jarring sound, growing increasingly tense as the wall clock ticked toward noon.

It wasn't that she disliked Jethro Weaver. He was a *gut* man. While measuring Gabriel's fabric to the length needed for his curtains, Hannah mentally listed the bishop's son's qualities. He was hardworking. He was quiet. He was… Smoothing the fabric, her lips quirked as she recalled Gabe's foolish description of what he was looking for. In fabric, or so he had said. In other things as well, she knew he had meant. It wasn't her. Not anymore. The scissors felt abnormally heavy when Hannah picked them up. She winced at the first snip.

It's what you have to do with him in your life. Cut him out. You've done it before, you can do it again. It didn't help that she hadn't heard the other sound her ear had been tuned for—the muted bang of the back door leading into the street—all morning. Was Gabe still upstairs in his apartment? Or had he already left for the day? Where was he?

She couldn't let it matter. She would do what was expected of her. That was the essence of *gelassenheit*. Yielding oneself to the will of a higher authority, be it *Gott*, the bishop or others, with contentment and a calm spirit was a core value of who they were as an Amish community. Hannah resolutely cut across the fabric. She needed to remember that she was beige. Not this vibrant blue.

What mattered now was Jethro. Who was hard-working. And reserved. And—she jumped, slashing the material jaggedly at the jarring bell announcing an arrival—here. Setting the scissors down, Hannah wiped her hands down the side of her skirt and stepped around the counter with a weak smile.

Jethro Weaver responded with a stiff nod as he shut the door. Hannah couldn't see his eyes below the flat brim of his black hat, but from the set of his jaw, evident even under his short beard, it looked as if he was as uncomfortable being there as she was having him there. Hannah wasn't sure if the realization made her feel better or worse. Allowing herself a last glance at the fabric on the counter and memory of the man who'd chosen it, she corrected herself. She couldn't feel much worse.

Injecting pleasant interest in her voice, she started for the door and the man standing rigidly beside it. "Mrs. Fastle should be back from lunch momentarily. When she arrives, we can go. Where did you have in mind?"

"The D-Dew D-Drop."

She'd forgotten Jethro had a stutter. When she got closer, Hannah could see the faint line of a scar perpendicular to his unsmiling upper lip. Standing just inside the door, they faced each other awkwardly. Jethro shuffled his feet. Hannah shifted hers. She was about to suggest he remove his coat while they waited when she heard the muffled bang of the door to the alley. Her heart jolted at the possibility that it was Gabe. Much more likely, it was announcing Barb's return. Stifling a sigh, as it meant she was now free to join the man before her for what would surely be an uncomfortable meal, Hannah reached for her black cloak and bonnet that hung on the nearby peg rack.

Hannah hissed in a breath when a smiling Gabe followed Barb through the shop's back door. Although he was chatting with her employer, his eyes scanned the shop until they locked with her own. Gabe's gaze shifted from her to the tall, lean man beside her and back again. Hannah found herself holding her breath until Gabe returned his attention to Barb. Fumbling the cloak off the peg, Hannah tossed it over her shoulders.

Nodding to Jethro to open the door, she called over her shoulder to her boss, "Now that you're back, I'll be going."

A cheery "Have a nice lunch!" followed them as they exited. Careful to keep a space between her and Jethro as they walked down the snow-dusted sidewalk, Hannah figured the best outcome she could hope for regarding the pending meal was for it to be tolerable.

Even that seemed unlikely when all heads turned in their direction as she and Jethro came through the door of Miller's Creek's main eating establishment. Hannah could almost tell from the ensuing expressions who was going to gossip about the two of them and who wasn't. By the time they sat down next to the window, she'd lost her appetite. Ordering a cup of soup, Hannah figured she might've agreed to the outing, but she didn't have to make it last long. She made a few feeble attempts at conversation, only to have Jethro nod or shake his head in response. When her soup arrived and he hadn't said a word other than to place his order, thoughts of three silent meals a day filled her heart with dread and her stomach with lead, prompting her to stir the soup more than eat it.

In the silence at her table, it was easy to listen to the conversation at the one behind her. Hannah stopped stirring at the words *stolen dog*. Straightening in her chair, she tipped her head back in order to hear what else was being said by the two *Englisch* diners.

"Found him down by Milwaukee. Wouldn't have if the new owners in the city hadn't taken him to the vet to be checked out and they discovered his microchip."

The other man grunted. "I'd heard some folks had dogs missing. Some mixed breeds, but mainly pure-breds. Mine raised a ruckus the other night. Since then, I make sure if she's outside, I am, too. So glad you got Ace returned. Scary to think of how many might not be. Do they have any idea who—"

Hannah jumped when the waitress stopped by to refill their coffee cups. Reluctantly tuning out the men behind her, she glanced over to Jethro. Fortunately for future silent meals, he seemed to be a fast eater. Hannah frowned down at her soup. *Easy to do, when you're not saying a word.* But, she reminded herself, conversation worked both ways. Hannah had a feeling this courtship wasn't his idea, either. She needed to make more of an attempt herself. Pasting on a smile, Hannah looked up, just in time to see Gabe walk into the restaurant.

"What's he doing here?" was not what she'd intended to ask the man across the table.

Jethro glanced over his shoulder to see Gabe closing the door. Raising his eyebrows, Jethro lifted his freshly filled coffee cup. "Eating?"

Hannah stirred her soup faster as heat flamed her ears, until she was tempted to tug her *kapp* down over what she knew would be their fiery red edges. It shouldn't have been a surprise that Gabe was there. Miller's Creek had few restaurants and The Dew Drop was the only one downtown. And she'd seen Gabe's kitchen, what there was of it. If he hadn't unpacked the boxes since yesterday, it would've been difficult for him to make even a sandwich in the apartment. No wonder he was eating all his meals here.

Still, Hannah almost groaned when Gabe sat in her line of sight. The restaurant was busy, but not so busy that he couldn't have sat somewhere else. She made a face when the young Amish waitress hurried over to him. Rebecca hadn't served their table that quickly.

"Your soup isn't *g-gut*?"

"*Nee*. The soup's fine." Hannah struggled not to stutter herself, caught as she was with her eyes and attention on another man and an alien twinge of jealousy racing through her. "Everything's fine." Keeping her gaze on Jethro, she strangled her spoon as Gabe laughed at something the pretty waitress said. At Jethro's furrowed brow, Hannah forced herself to take a bite of the baked potato soup in front of her. "Can't beat hot soup on a cold day."

Raising his sandy-blond eyebrows again at the congealing mixture in her cup, Jethro swiveled in his chair to take another look at the man seated behind him. Now heat infused Hannah's cheeks until she was sure they were hotter than the soup had ever been as the two men nodded stiffly to each other. Jethro swung back to regard her quizzically. Under the intense regard of both men, the heat crept down her neck. Determinedly, she took another bite. As she chewed the lumpy mass, Hannah struggled to push up the corners of her mouth into what she hoped was a friendly smile. They felt heavier than the bales of hay that she helped her *brieder* load on wagons in the summer.

Scooping up another bite, she winced at the sound of the spoon scraping the crockery. She had no interest in food. But if eating while watching the flirtation across the room curbed her misplaced hunger for a life with the man sitting there, it was worth forcing it down.

The approaching waitress was a needed distraction as Gabe tried not to stare at Hannah.

"What can I get you today?" she asked cheerfully, the smile on her lips matching the one in her eyes.

You can get the man sitting by Hannah to move to another table. Gabe's own smile was a trial to keep in place. "The daily special sounds good." He'd eaten at the restaurant several times already. Usually he enjoyed his interactions with the pretty waitress. Not today.

Rebecca laughed. "I haven't told you what it is yet."

"Doesn't matter. Anything The Dew Drop makes is good." It was true. But Gabe knew anything he'd eat today would be tasteless with Hannah sitting across the room with another man. An Amish man and an unmarried Amish woman didn't normally sit together unless something was going on. The only thing that gave Gabe a smidgen of peace was that the man had a beard. In the Plain world, that meant he was already married.

"Pretty good crowd today," he observed, making a point to look around the room as Rebecca topped his water glass off for the second time. "I'm getting to know by face a number of folks in town, but have a ways to go yet. For example, the couple next to the window? I've seen the woman at the quilt shop below my apartment, but I'm not familiar with the man."

The waitress swiveled to see where he was looking. "Oh, that's Hannah Lapp. She's worked for the shop's *Englisch* owner for a number of years." Her gaze sharpened at the sight of the man. "She's sitting with Jethro Weaver, the bishop's son. Poor man just lost his wife and unborn child about a month ago."

Gabe nodded stiffly when the man turned to look at him. He remembered the case. Tragic indeed. The gossip was the woman had suffered a stroke, probably from eclampsia. So heartbreaking, as the condition was preventable. But sometimes Amish women didn't always seek prenatal care, at least until later months of their pregnancy.

From what he'd understood, the awful incident had helped push the grant responsible for his job through. "Time is tissue" was a mantra in the EMS world. Prompt help increased positive outcomes. A factor that Gabe was all too familiar with.

A cold burst of air swept over the table. Needing to distract himself from the pair at the window, Gabe glanced toward the door to see the bishop and his wife, whom he'd already had pointed out to him, come through it. The older couple scanned the room before pausing in their apparent search, a smug look settling over both their thin faces. Gabe followed their gazes to where Hannah and the bishop's son sat. From the Weavers' faces, the sight of the two together was met with a great deal of satisfaction. The younger couple's relationship was obviously an arranged match.

Gabe's mouth went dry. Leaning back in the booth, he pushed the plate Rebecca had set in from of him off to the side, his appetite suddenly gone.

Rebecca stopped by his booth again, water pitcher in hand. Her smile drooped a little when she saw the rejected plate. "Is everything all right?"

"Everything's just fine," he murmured, looking at the couple across the restaurant. Gabe knew, in order to convince Hannah to marry him, he already needed to overcome whatever had spooked her from their deepening relationship years earlier. Now he'd be confronting the will of the community's leader. The community he knew was important to the woman he loved.

Persuading Hannah that they belonged together seemed impossible.

Chapter Four

The truck rocked to a stop in front of a team of draft horses. The Belgians jerked up their heads when Gabe flung open the door. A quick glance behind the team revealed a wagon of cut lumber. One end of the load was unsecured, with boards sliding from the wagon to rest on the ground. Snagging his jump bag from the passenger seat, Gabe was a step away from the cab before the last rumble of the truck's engine faded on the crisp winter morning.

Bounding through the foot-deep snow in the ditch, he climbed over the barbed wire fence. His eyes stayed focused on the figures gathered at the edge of a small pond in the cow pasture beyond.

"Is he out?" he called as he ran, crunching across the snow-crusted grass loosely braided with cattle paths.

"Ben's got him!"

Dodging through the handful of youngsters clustered anxiously along the pond's bank, he saw an Amish man, garbed in a dark coat and watch cap, holding on to a rope. Gabe's sharp gaze followed the line across the frozen pond, its surface splintered with cracks like a broken windshield, to another man sprawled on the ice. This man's dark hair was plastered to his head, his arm hooked over a boy's chest. The youth sagged against the man's blue coat. His head bounced gently with each jerk of the rope as the Amish man pulled it in. An ominous crackle and pop drew gasps from the boys as another long splinter appeared on the pond's surface next to the prone pair. Gabe grabbed the icy rope and heaved in sync with the man.

"Did he go under?"

"Ja."

"How long?"

"About five minutes before Ben pulled him out."

"You know the kid?"

"Nee. He's *Englisch.*"

The pair was sliding closer to the ragged brown weeds that fringed the pond. "Hey, kids!" Gabe called to the hovering crowd of boys. "What's your friend's name?"

"Alex," one of the older boys responded shakily. "Is he going to be okay?"

"We'll do everything we can," Gabe assured him, although his stomach clenched at the sight of the boy's limp figure. *Keep calm, Bartel. Maybe you can save this one.* His muscles strained with another coordinated pull on the line. "What happened?"

"It looked like a good place to play hockey. Then we heard a crash, and Alex went down. We tried to get to him, but the ice was popping and we thought we all might go under, so we got off. Derek called 911 and when we saw these guys coming… We should have gone out there to help him." The boy's voice started to crack.

"Nah. You did good. Otherwise we'd be pulling more of you out." Gabe's attention was on the pair, close enough now to reach from the frozen ground of the bank. Both man and boy were white-faced, the boy's lips growing bluer as Gabe watched. Reaching out a hand, the Amish rescuer assisted his friend off the ice. Rivulets of water ran from the other man's dark hair, streaming down over his face as he tried to lift the boy toward Gabe.

"That's okay. I got him." Snagging his jump bag, Gabe swept the limp boy into his arms, the sopping blond head lolling over his elbow. Working his way over the jagged terrain to the first flat ground he could find, Gabe gently laid the boy on his back. The kid wasn't breathing. He pressed fingers to the cold skin of the boy's neck. Nothing. No chest movement. No faint throbbing under his fingertips to indicate the kid was still alive. Gabe's own heart was pounding like he'd been thrashing in icy waters. Quickly snagging a CPR mask, he adjusted it over the boy's face.

"Stay with me, Alex," he muttered as he positioned himself over the motionless form. Without conscious thought, he began chest compressions to the rhythmic beat of an old disco tune. Thirty compressions, two quick breaths, back to the compressions, the process was automatic. Two minutes into the sequence, Gabe checked again for a pulse. Still nothing. "Come on, Alex," he begged, resuming compressions.

For a moment, the scenery surrounding Gabe shifted from frozen water and snow-skiffed earth to one lush and green. The slack face below him was not an unknown boy, but his well-loved little brother.

Only muscle memory kept Gabe's rhythm from breaking. But he had to draw in a shuddering gasp before he could breathe for himself, much less for the boy.

One of the two men hovering tensely nearby shifted. Gabe welcomed the distraction. "How'd you get here so fast?"

The dry one, blond hair curling up from under his dark blue watch cap, responded. "We were taking a load of lumber to the furniture shop in town. Heard the boys calling. Ben cut the rope on the load and we used it as a line in case he went down with the boy. Which he did. I think intentionally."

Gabe glanced up while he continued pressing the heels of his hands against the boy's chest. The Amish man's words might've been flippant, but his face was strained. Gabe followed the man's concerned gaze when it shifted to his companion.

The dark-haired man was shaking under his wet coat. "He went under." The words were barely audible due to his chattering teeth. Gabe's brow lowered at the sight of the man's pinched, white face.

"Ben, right?" After Gabe gave the boy two more breaths and resumed compressions, he shot another look at the man crouched beside him.

"Ja."

Gabe couldn't tell if the man responded with a nod or was just shaking. "I can't take care of both of you. Get in my truck. Can you turn it on? Good. Start it up and get the heater going. Behind the seat I have an extra jacket. Take off your wet clothes and put it on. Hopefully by then the ambulance will have arrived and you can fill them in when you bring them over here. Got it? Good."

"Nothing yet?" the blond man asked, watching his friend stumble across the field toward the truck.

"Nobody is dead until they're warm and dead," Gabe panted in time with the compressions. "You know CPR?" He grunted in relief at the man's hesitant nod. After giving the boy two more quick breaths, he checked again for a pulse. Nothing. Resuming compressions, Gabe hoped the sound in his ears was the faint wail of the ambulance and not encroaching fatigue. Or the memory of a brother he couldn't save. *Please, God, no. Don't let me lose another one.*

Hannah hesitantly tapped on the apartment's door. Holding her breath, she listened for the sound of someone crossing the floor to respond to her knock. At the continued silence, she rapped again, slightly louder. With no ensuing footfalls as the seconds passed, her shoulders sagged. Hannah told herself it was with relief, not disappointment. Gabe was still out.

She'd thought she'd heard him leave earlier in the day. *Who are you trying to fool, Hannah Lapp? You're aware of every single sound that comes from this apartment. I'm surprised you don't hear the dust settling. You know he left thirty minutes after you arrived this morning and hasn't come back yet.*

Hannah winced at the guilt that bounced through her head like popcorn on a hot stove. She hadn't seen Gabe since her uncomfortable meal at The Dew Drop earlier that week. She'd finished his curtains at home last night. Her *mamm* had regarded her curiously when Hannah awkwardly explained what she was making, but hadn't said anything further. Hannah had wanted to get the curtains done quickly and to not have a reason to think about him…*them* anymore.

Which didn't explain the extra care she'd taken to ensure they were some of her best work. Or the fact that when she'd heard his tread on the stairs and the thud of the back door this morning, she'd battled briefly with dismay that he'd left before she could get upstairs to hang them. She was glad he'd be gone when she went upstairs with the curtains and the rods Barb had provided. Wasn't she? It was only because she'd been busy with customers and other duties that she hadn't been able to get upstairs to take care of it while he was out. Not because she'd been hoping he'd return before she went up.

Which he hadn't. With a sigh, Hannah tentatively twisted the door knob and entered the apartment.

Gabe had been right. He hadn't collected much in the way of household goods. The apartment was Spartan beyond a tired couch, bordered by a scuffed wooden coffee table and worn end tables. The simple mismatched collection faced an oil-burning stove. Hannah glanced at the blue material in her hands and smiled wryly. He'd also been right that the apartment needed some cheering up.

Closing the door behind her, Hannah headed for the window, making note of every detail of the room. It wasn't because it was his. She was just curious. That was all. She wrinkled her nose as her feet echoed on the wooden floor. A rug would warm up the room both in appearance and functionality. Pursing her lips, Hannah recalled some old wool her *mamm* had been keeping for years. Perhaps she'd let Hannah have it to braid a rug, just a little one, to lie between the couch and coffee table. Just something warm he could put his feet on over the winter—

Shrieking, Hannah clutched the curtains to her chest at the sight of the body lying on the floor beyond the couch. Staring at the motionless figure, she froze. It took a few frantic heartbeats for her to realize it wasn't a body…exactly. Although the yellow hair was almost lifelike, the rigid face beneath it obviously was not. The blue sweatshirt on the—Man? Woman? Doll?—was zipped up to just under a plastic chin.

Still, she backed away from the lifeless form. When she reached the window, following one last look to ensure the figure didn't move, she pivoted. Setting the rods and curtains at the base, Hannah looked up at the tall window. Realizing she didn't have any nails to attach the rod's brackets to the wall or a hammer to secure them, Hannah wrinkled her nose in dismay. *It's no wonder, you* dummkopf. *You were more concerned with the missing man than the job at hand.*

Keeping a wary eye on the body at the end of the couch, Hannah headed for the door. And shrieked again when it swung open toward her. The heavy beat of her heart thrummed under her fingertips as she clutched her chest. Gabe swept through the door and jerked it closed, his alarmed green eyes touching on her before they scrutinized the rest of the small apartment. Ascertaining no threat, he frowned and set down the black backpack in his hand. Closing the distance between them, he gently curled his hands around her upper arms. "Are you all right?"

"*Ja.* I just wasn't expecting you to come through the door."

As Gabe searched her face, his gaze gradually softened its intensity. His fingers twitched on her arms and, for a moment, it seemed he would draw her to him. Hannah held her breath. When Gabe relaxed his hold and stepped away, she let it out in a quiet sigh. *Surely not of disappointment?*

With a furrowed brow, Gabe glanced around the apartment again before returning his attention to Hannah, his cheek creasing at the slight lift in the corner of his mouth. "What are you doing up here?"

Her own cheeks heating, Hannah closed her eyes in frustration. *I was going to be calm when I saw him again. In control. Distantly pleasant, as should a woman be who is going to marry another man. Not screeching throughout his apartment like a startled owl. Or trembling like a leaf in a breeze when he touches me.* Opening her eyes, she gestured uncomfortably toward the window before crossing her arms in front of her. "I finished your curtains. I was going to hang them, but I didn't have all the tools I needed."

Shrugging off his coat, Gabe hung it on a peg on the wall before he looked toward the stack of blue fabric lying under the window. "Oh," he said distractedly. He smiled at her. But it wasn't the teasing, personal smile that'd originally drawn her to him at the party years ago. It didn't involve his eyes that Hannah knew could dance like a flame in a fireplace. If her behavior was different than she'd envisioned, his was dramatically so. *What was going on?*

Crossing to the window with a heavy tread, Gabe picked up the curtains. Staring down at the blue fabric, he absently stroked his hand over the top of the stack. "They're beautiful. They'll really brighten up the place. Thank you." His normally rich baritone barely deviated from a monotone.

Something was definitely wrong. Hannah frowned. Arms still folded, she trailed after him to the window. "I almost decorated your apartment by tossing them in the air to land willy-nilly. And stabbing myself in with the rods in the process."

"What?" Gabe turned to her, with sharper attention in his gaze.

"I was afraid you'd committed a murder up here and I'd discovered the body."

He lowered the hand holding the curtains, the material tumbling down his side to look like he was dangling a rich blue cape. "What?" he repeated.

At least she'd broken through his stupor. Whatever'd been bothering him, she'd succeeded in cracking through its disturbing hold on the man. Unfolding her arms, Hannah pointed to the end of the couch. "That thing over there."

His gaze followed the direction of her finger. "Oh—" a little bit of Gabe's normally endearing smile twitched on his lips "—Annie."

"It has a name?"

"Oh, yeah. Rescue Annie, CPR Annie, Resuscitation Annie, or simply Resusci Annie. She and I are old buddies." His smile expanded. "Currently, she's my only partner."

Now it was Hannah's turn to be a little startled. "What?"

Gathering up the material, Gabe refolded it before setting it against the wall. He strode over, more enthusiasm in his step now, toward the form at the end of the couch. He picked up the doll, its legs dangling below the stiff chest. "I teach CPR. Cardiopulmonary resuscitation. If you can keep the heart going, you have a chance to keep someone alive. If a person's heart stops, or they stop breathing, CPR manually pumps blood to the vital organs of the body until it can get started again. Or until it's determined…" Gabe's legs seemed to give out from under him. Clasping the mannequin, he sank down onto the couch.

"There was a boy today. A drowning. He was gone. I didn't know if we could get him back. He was the same age as…" Gabe pressed his lips together for a moment. "As I was doing CPR, all I could see was Will. Will's face. Will's blue lips. Will's slack body that I couldn't bring back." Gabe's voice was barely audible with his last words. One tear, followed shortly by another, tracked down the edge of his nose to drip onto on the doll's blue shirt.

Shaken, and gripped with the need to comfort him, Hannah found herself seated beside him. The worn cushion sagged, tipping her toward Gabe. She reached out a hand to his upper arm, both to console him and to brace herself from drifting in farther. "Will?" she whispered.

Gabe's hands clenched on the mannequin, his knuckles showing white for a moment before they relaxed their grip. "Will was my little brother." He exhaled deeply, his shoulders sagging with the action. "He drowned. I was preoccupied with…things. By the time I noticed he was…" He stared at the scarred wooden floor at his feet. "It was too late. I hadn't paid much attention in high school health class the day we did CPR. I mean, who really expects to use that?" His

throat worked in a hard swallow. "If I had, maybe…"
He bowed his head.

Hannah's own eyes prickled with tears. She rubbed
her hand lightly over the blue sleeve covering his bicep,
wanting to soothe. "When did this happen? You'd mentioned a little *bruder* when we were together, but you
never said…"

When Gabe didn't respond, Hannah figured he
wasn't going to answer her question. When he did,
she wished he hadn't.

"It was shortly after you didn't show up that night. I
didn't know how to find you. It wasn't like we'd been
seen together, so I could go asking around the Amish
folks. I did a bit." He snorted softly. "You can imagine
what kind of reception I got. After a while, I figured
if you'd wanted to see me, you would have. So I went
home to Madison that weekend, trying to forget you. Or
at least trying to understand what might've happened to
make you disappear. I thought we…" His voice died off.

Squeezing her eyes shut to keep her tears at bay,
Hannah recalled her own grief when she'd known she
had to break off their relationship. She hadn't thought
of him. *How selfish of me.* Her fingers tightened on
his arm. Gabe's eyes remained focused on the scarred
wooden floor in front of the couch.

"To distract myself, I decided to go swimming at
a local lake my family frequented. My little brother
wanted to come along. As we'd been there before, I
figured, sure, why not." His lips twisted. "I went out
into the deeper water. I was swimming hard, trying to
forget… Will tried to follow me. When I finally looked
around, he was gone. I—I found him, but I couldn't

bring him back." Gabe tipped his head to the back of the worn couch and closed his eyes.

"I dropped out of school up here. Went back home for the rest of the semester to be with my folks. That fall, I changed my major. If I couldn't save Will, at least I could learn to save others." He exhaled in a shuddering sigh. "Today it helped me save the boy, Alex."

Wrung out just listening to his excruciating tale, Hannah remained rooted in her position on the couch. Knowing she played a part in it filled her with sorrow that couldn't be extinguished by tears. She swallowed against the swelling in her throat.

In their time together, she'd known Gabe as a fun and interesting companion. A caring, considerate man who'd made her laugh. She'd known joy with him, unlike anything she'd felt with anyone else. Enough that she'd almost left everything she'd known to be with him. In their interactions, she hadn't seen this depth of compassion. Her heart ached for him. It felt odd, yet right to be the one to comfort him. But how?

"Praise God for the two guys that beat me there today. They were Amish. Maybe you know them?" Opening his eyes, Gabe lifted his head to look at her. "Apparently they work for the furniture company in town. Gideon Schrock spelled me for a bit on CPR before the ambulance got there. A guy named Ben Raber went into the pond after the kid. They were amazing. It was their quick thinking more than my actions that saved the day. Good men. Said they're on the volunteer fire department. I look forward to working with them."

Hannah knew she needed to respond, but wasn't sure how. He needed her. How could she assuage and distract him from his grief? She latched on to the last things he'd said.

"I've known Ben most of my life. Gideon moved in a year or so ago." Clearing her throat, she forced emotions she didn't feel into her voice. "Are you telling me Ben can do something I can't? And if Gideon knows, then in all likelihood, my new brother-in-law Samuel Schrock knows how to do it, as well. And he'd never let me live that down. I don't suppose you could show me how to do this CPR thing on…Annie, was it?"

Gabe regarded her doubtfully. "You really want to learn?"

"Of course! Assuming you're a *gut* teacher."

His eyes began to dance in the way Hannah realized she treasured. His lips hooked in a half smile. "I haven't lost a mannequin yet."

"Let's see if you can keep it that way." Gabe's gaze traveled from her smiling face to where her hand still lightly rested on his upper arm. Jerking it away, Hannah clasped it in her lap.

Annie under one arm, Gabe agilely pushed up from the couch and turned to offer his hand to assist Hannah. "These old cushions have made it a possessive couch. Once you're in it, it doesn't want to let you go."

Her fingers still humming from their contact with his muscular bicep and her sensibilities from his unexpected vulnerability, Hannah smiled, but avoided touching him. She could relate to the couch's sentiments in regard to the man in front of her. It'd been difficult to let him go. Wedging an elbow against the arm of the worn sofa, she levered herself out.

"While doing CPR, you want the person on their

back on a firm surface." Gabe laid the mannequin in the middle of the wooden floor and knelt beside it. "You're going to regret not making me pillows," he commented, with a rueful look at the scarred floor. The look he shot Hannah acknowledged there were other things in their relationship that he was regretting, as well.

So was Hannah. She was regretting that she couldn't wrap her arms around his neck to comfort him. To stroke a gentle finger over a furrowed brow. To brush a kiss on his wind-tousled hair. To ask more about a little *bruder* whom he'd obviously loved very much. But they didn't have that kind of relationship. They couldn't. But that didn't mean Hannah's heart didn't ache for Gabe's loss. That she didn't love… Hannah stepped back from the thought, bumping into the couch and almost sinking into it again.

Gabe wanting to help people was very noble. It was admiration she felt. That was all. Hannah thought of her own young *brieder*. She couldn't imagine them being in danger because of her and failing to help them. If teaching her CPR diminished the pain from Gabe's eyes…

Briskly, Hannah circled the mannequin and knelt on its other side. "At home, our floor is covered with linoleum. It's not much softer. What should I do?"

"Hmm," Gabe regarded her across the blue-shirted figure. "There's a bit to it, but it's not difficult. If you're really interested, I can see about having you attend the volunteer firefighters' training meeting tomorrow evening. I'm re-certifying them on CPR. So for now, I'm just going to give you the basics, which can still help you save a life. Lack of oxygenated blood can cause brain damage within a few minutes. A person can die within eight to ten. CPR keeps that blood moving."

Hannah was afraid to ask, but she wanted to know. "What about the boy today?"

Gabe smiled slightly. "Time will tell, but praise God, it was looking good when I left the hospital."

Hannah couldn't prevent her corresponding grin. "*Gut.* I'm glad."

Her breath caught when Gabe didn't look away. Shifting, he leaned fractionally closer. Pulled by a seemingly invisible thread Hannah edged forward. Lowering a hand to brace him, Gabe flinched when the heel of it pressed into Annie's chest. Abruptly straightening, he sank back.

"Okay, the first thing you want to be aware of when you come upon someone needing aid is BSI, body substance isolation, and scene safety. Kind of a problem doing chest compressions on a person if you're surrounded by fire or in the middle of a road and could get hit by a car."

Hannah's eyes rounded.

"So check to see if the surroundings are safe. Then determine if the person is conscious." Gabe glanced at Hannah to see if she followed. At her nod, he continued, "If they're unconscious, tap them or shake their shoulder and ask, 'Are you okay?'" Annie wiggled under his hand as Gabe's loud voice echoed around the small apartment.

"You try now."

Feeling a little silly, Hannah did as he instructed.

"If you don't get any response, you need to take

immediate action. If you're with someone, have them call 911." Gabe sat back on his heels as he regarded her. "Which might be difficult in your community. Although, come to think of it, a number of your youth carry cell phones during their *rumspringa*. Well, if you're with someone, have them get to a phone and dial 911 to get help. If you're alone and you have a phone close, make the call before you start compressions. If you don't have a phone close and you're alone, go straight into chest compressions. Got it?"

Knowing he expected some response from her, Hannah nodded weakly. It was a lot to think about.

"Okay, the normal acronym is C-A-B. The C stands for compressions, which is keeping the blood circulating. The A is airway. Open the airway. The B is for breathing. You have to breathe for the person."

Her concern must have shown, as Gabe paused. "Hmm. Yeah, well, for you, we're just going to teach chest compressions. Keep doing them until there's movement or someone else can take over. Compressions may still keep someone alive until help arrives. If you want to learn more, come tomorrow night."

"Ah, I think this will be enough. I, um, wouldn't want to show them up with my new skills."

"I understand." From the way Gabe looked at her, she knew he also understood why she was doing this. Understood and was grateful. Hannah's pulse accelerated. She couldn't look away. *What happens when you're breathless and your heart is pounding too hard? Is there something that's the opposite of CPR to assist with that before you make a fool of yourself?*

Blinking dazedly, Gabe glanced down at Annie.

"Um, let's see." He pointed to where the material of Hannah's skirt almost brushed the mannequin's shoulder. "You're kneeling in the right position." He unzipped the doll's blue jacket to expose the plastic chest. "Now, place the heel of one hand over the center of the person's chest right here." He placed his hand in the center of the mannequin's chest, right above the V indicating the end of the rib cage. "Then put your other hand on top of the first hand. Like so." He demonstrated. "Make sure your shoulders are directly above your hands and keep your elbows straight. Now you try."

Gabe retreated. Hannah leaned forward to hesitantly put the heel of her palm against Annie's cool, hard plastic. She placed her other hand on top of it.

"Just a little farther over here." Gabe reached out to gently shift her position and adjust her fingers. Hannah froze at the warm touch of his hands enveloping hers. Breathlessly, she glanced up to meet Gabe's eyes. They were equally shaken. His fingers flexed on hers a moment before he drew in a ragged breath and shifted away. "That's…it. Right there."

And it was. The unexplained, unanticipated, incomparable feeling that'd happened the first time their hands had touched.

Gabe cleared his throat. He reached out as if he was going to touch her shoulders to reposition her before thinking better of it. "Okay, elbows straight, and shoulders directly over your hands. That's good."

Flushing under his praise, Hannah composed a bland, interested expression as she sat back.

Gabe repositioned himself over the mannequin.

"You can't use just your arms, you have to use your upper body weight. Push straight down on the chest about two inches."

Wincing, Hannah bit her lip. It seemed so much.

"Remember, you are beating their heart for them. You're saving their life. Believe me, if their heart isn't beating, they'd rather you do it than not." He demonstrated. "You want to do compressions at a rate of 100 to 120 per minute." He hooked a smile at her. "I don't suppose you listen to a lot of music?"

Frowning, Hannah shook her head.

"Well, there was a song that came out during the disco craze that has the perfect beat. It's called, ironically, 'Stayin' Alive.'"

"Was the song written for CPR?"

"No," he laughed softly, "but it fits." He sat back again. "You try now."

Hannah positioned herself over Annie, careful to put her hands in the correct position. She tentatively pressed down, surprised at the give of the mannequin. Rebounding, she pressed again.

"You got it. Now a little faster."

Hannah picked up the speed of her compressions.

"That's it. Now take it from the top. You find a person unresponsive."

Hannah went through the steps, pleased she remembered them all, ending with a minute of compressions. Strong as she knew herself to be from helping with farm work, she was surprised at how fatiguing CPR could be. She was slightly winded when she looked over to see Gabe nodding in satisfaction.

"I know. An untrained person can usually last about

ten to fifteen minutes doing CPR. You did great. Do you want more?"

Hannah knew he only meant further training. She needed to get back downstairs. Away from him, away from the truth that she wanted so much more from him. She wanted to be able to give so much more. Her hand, her heart, her life to share with him. But that would mean giving up her community and opening her parents to more pain. Which she couldn't do. The most she could get from and give to Gabe was a careful friendship.

Shaking her head, she cleared her throat awkwardly. "*Denki* for the lesson. Now I can hold my head up around Ben, Gideon and Samuel. But I pray I never have to use it."

"My pleasure. And you won't be the first one leaving a CPR class with that thought."

As Hannah rose to her feet, she noticed the splash of blue against the wall. "The curtains! I was going to hang them for you. If you'll give me a moment, I'll run down for a hammer and some nails to hang the rods."

Gabe picked up the mannequin and returned it to the end of the couch. "I've unpacked recently enough that I remember where I put mine. I'll help you."

Within minutes, they had the rods and curtains up. Gabe had been correct. They certainly brightened up the place. As did the smile that Gabe now wore. Trotting downstairs, Hannah couldn't deny the pleasure she felt in knowing she'd put it there. Her descent slowed as she realized that even though she'd never stopped loving Gabriel Bartel, she was still going to marry another man.

Chapter Five

Gabe turned off the highway onto the country road. It wasn't exactly out of the way. Okay, it was a bit out of the way, but he was going to take this route on his return from teaching an early-morning CPR recertification class at the Portage hospital. If the route just happened to go past Hannah's farm, which he'd recently discovered the address of, well, a critical part of his job involved being able to quickly find locations in the county. Surely it made sense to explore his new area?

Perhaps knowing where Hannah lived might prevent her from disappearing from his life again. Although, Gabe mused that not knowing her address didn't rate high now among their obstacles. But while Hannah had learned a bit about CPR yesterday, Gabe had learned that she wasn't indifferent to him. There might still be reason to maintain a sliver of hope for their relationship. What could he say, he was a hopeful guy.

Gabe slowed as he passed her family's pristine farm

yard, raising his eyebrows as he noted clothes on the line, even on a cold winter morning. But the pants and dresses shifting in the slight breeze were the only movement at the farm. What had he expected? Just because it was her day off didn't mean she'd spend it outside so he could see her as he drove by.

Turning at the next corner, he frowned at the sight of a black-cloaked figure walking on the side of the road some distance ahead. As the truck slowed, his heartbeat increased as he knew, without seeing the Amish woman's face, it was Hannah. He lowered the window as the vehicle rolled along at the quick pace of the woman beside it.

"Do you need a ride?" When she turned to him, Gabe's smile immediately disappeared at the sight of her face. Jabbing the brakes, he slammed the truck into Park. A second later, he was out the door and wrapping his arms about her unresisting form. "What's wrong?"

Red-faced in spite of the cold, Hannah was obviously striving for composure. Gabe rubbed her back in slow circles as he felt her hiccupping breaths. "Socks is missing," she got out in a high, tight voice. Like a dam breaking, her face crumpled and she began to sob. Gabe pulled her more tightly into an embrace, gently rocking her back and forth as he felt hot tears against his neck.

Gabe knew what the Border collie meant to her. "How long?"

He could barely make out the words that were spoken into his shoulder in between sharp inhalations. "She disappeared when I let her out last night. I heard a few sharp barks, but I didn't think anything of it as she and Dash sometimes play. When I went looking for her, I found Dash with my folks in the barn for milking, and Socks was gone. I wanted to search last night, but *Daed* discouraged me from going out in the dark." Gabe's arms tightened about her as Hannah's slender shoulders shook with renewed sobs.

"Shh. It'll be okay. We'll find her." Gabe rested his chin on the wool of her black bonnet. "Have you seen any sign of her along the road?"

"N-No. I've been looking since daylight. What if she was stuck in a fence and couldn't get to me? What if she fell through the ice like that boy? What if someone t-took her?" Hannah tipped her head back. Gabe's heart almost broke at the misery in her blue eyes.

Unwrapping one arm from around her, Gabe wiped a tear from her cheek. "We'll keep looking. But you won't do her any good by freezing before you find her." He shepherded her to the other side of the truck. "Get in. We can cover more ground this way. We'll go slow and keep the windows cracked so you can call and listen."

Upon assisting Hannah into the vehicle, Gabe quickly returned to the driver's side, climbed in and turned up the heat. They continued slowly down the country road with Hannah intermittently calling for Socks in an increasingly quavering voice before straining to listen for any responding bark over the quiet rumble of the engine. When they reached the first lane, Gabe stopped and turned to Hannah, who sat forlornly in the passenger seat.

"You want me to go in and ask? I can check to see if they've heard anything."

Hannah looked up the lane to the large white house before shifting her gaze to his face. "It's Amish," she murmured.

"I know." He regarded her solemnly. "Still, much is lost for want of asking. If they know something about Socks, it might be worth it." Gabe ached for her, though. Being seen with a young man from outside her community was an issue for Hannah. In hindsight, he'd realized the unintentional covertness of their previous meetings had probably contributed to her disappearance years ago. If they had any chance for a relationship now, it had to be held out in the open. Gabe kept himself from trying to persuade her further. Since the risk was hers, the decision had to be hers, as well.

His heart rate rocketed, and he found it hard to breathe when Hannah reached out a hand to where his rested on the console. "All right."

Rotating his hand, they entwined fingers. Gabe turned into the lane. When they parked in front of the house, he gave her hand a squeeze before reluctantly releasing it. "We'll find her."

But they didn't find her there. The Amish woman who came to the door hadn't seen a Border collie. She made sure they knew she didn't like seeing Hannah traveling with an *Englisch*.

When Gabe returned to the truck, Hannah had tugged her black cloak more closely about her and kept her hands in her lap. Her eyes glistened with tears and her mouth trembled. "She's a neighborhood gossip. Everyone will know."

"Good, that way everyone knows we're looking for your dog, so if they see Socks, they'll contact you."

Hannah's smile was weak, but her eyes were grateful for his support. "Maybe."

They stopped at three more houses, two Amish and one *Englisch*, before turning onto the highway. The woman at one Amish home was neutral, but curious. The man's gaze at the other had shifted repeatedly between Gabe and where Hannah remained in the truck during the brief conversation. No one had seen Socks.

Hannah sat in the passenger seat, head bowed, silently weeping. "I don't think she would have come this far."

Gabe handed her some napkins from his stash in the console. "Well, there's one way to find out." He pulled into the first lane off the highway. They heard a dog barking before they were halfway up it. Jerking up her head, Hannah shot Gabe a wide-eyed look.

"Could be any," he cautioned her.

"I know that bark." Hannah's hand was on the door latch before he braked to a halt. Her door bounced on its hinges as she jumped out to rush for a fenced-in backyard, the source of the barking. Before she could reach it, a black-and-white dog scrambled over the fence and raced toward her. With a sob, Hannah crumpled to the ground, the dog leaping into her arms. Exiting the truck, Gabe watched as Socks licked Hannah's face exuberantly.

As he walked up the concrete steps, a gray-haired *Englisch* woman opened the door, dish towel in her hand. "I'm so glad someone came for her. She's too sweet of a dog not to have come from a loving home. Wondered if she was from the Amish community. Anyway, glad you found her."

Frowning, Gabe turned his head to look at the joyous reunion. "She's usually wearing a collar."

The woman shook her head. "There wasn't a collar on her when we found her early this morning. Only a rope with a short tail. Looked like it might've been gnawed through. I took it off her. You want it?"

"Thanks. I'd like to see it if you don't mind."

The woman disappeared to return a moment later, a rope with a knotted loop on one end and a frayed braid on the other in her hand. Examining it, Gabe agreed with her assessment. Socks had been tied up somewhere and chewed her way free. But where? And by whom?

Returning his attention to the woman, Gabe opened his mouth to thank her, only to be forestalled when she fixed her attention on his name tag and trailed it down over his shirt and the blue pants common to his profession.

"Are you that new paramedic guy that came with the grant? Sure glad that came through. Saw in the local paper that there were some issues with it, though. Hopefully they can get those resolved. Never know what's going to happen when county administrations change."

Gabe just nodded. He'd heard the rumors, as well. Maybe that's why the old guard had been so quick to hire him in. His stomach clenched at the thought of what he'd do if the grant fell through. With another polite nod for the loquacious woman, he looked over to see Hannah's smile as she rested her cheek on Socks's head. Any concern for himself evaporated in relief at having her reunited with her dog.

"So you'd be the one that saved the Winston boy? He lives just down the road. That would've been such a tragedy. Can't imagine the heartache in this neighborhood if you weren't there."

Gabe shook his head, wanting to be sure she knew who deserved the credit. "Some Amish men on the volunteer fire department got him out first. The boy owes his life more to them than me."

The woman nodded. "Some folks around here aren't sure about the Amish. Don't like to see them buying up the land. I imagine the feelings might be mutual. Human nature, I guess. I think the Amish have been good neighbors to us. Polite. Hardworking. Now who's this, so I know who to contact if that lovely dog shows up again?"

"This is Hannah Lapp. She lives around the corner, down the road. The dog is Socks."

"I'm Cindy Borders." She firmly shook Gabe's hand. "You ever need anything, just let me know."

Hannah was coming up the steps, Socks following closely at her heels. *"Denki."*

The woman smiled. "You're welcome."

Gabe turned to Hannah. "You ready to go?"

Waving to Mrs. Borders, they returned to the truck. When Hannah motioned Socks to get into the cab, the collie backed away.

Gabe raised his eyebrows at the dog's behavior. "You ever have that issue with her before?"

Hannah shook her head. *"Nee.* Not that I'm aware of. She doesn't ride in many trucks, but she jumps right into the buggy."

"Hmm." Gabe wondered if it had something to do

with the dog's disappearance. "Get in. I'll hand her to you."

Moments later, Gabe settled into his seat to find Hannah with her arms around her dog, regarding him from across the console. "Gabe. I can't thank you enough for helping me find her."

He gripped the steering wheel with both hands to keep himself from reaching for her. Didn't Hannah know how he felt about her? That he was still hoping they could marry and have a lifetime together? If not, should he tell her? Hadn't he acknowledged that if there was a chance for their relationship, they had to bring things out into the open? Hoping he wasn't making a mistake, he drew in a deep breath and turned to meet her appreciative gaze. "It was my pleasure. Truly. You know I'd do anything to make you happy, Hannah. Except leave. I can't do that. Not when I think there's a chance for us."

Hannah's mouth dropped open, and she blinked rapidly. For a moment, as he'd recently witnessed it when they'd found Socks, Gabe recognized pure joy on her face. His breathing stilled. He leaned closer, reaching his hand toward her when the *clip-clop* of hooves on the pavement cut through the crisp weather. Hannah looked toward the highway, her profile blocked by the brim of her black bonnet.

When she looked back, her beautiful face was as frozen as the ice in some of the farmyard's winter puddles. Ignoring his outstretched hand, she shifted in her seat to be as close to the passenger door as possible. The Border collie immediately put her front paws in Hannah's lap and stuck her head out the window as

Gabe drove down the lane. A horse and buggy passed when they reached the end of it, the driver and his passenger peering at the truck through the windshield.

As they pulled out and the hoof beats faded away, the ensuing silence in the truck cab was uncomfortable. Striving not to feel dejected, Gabe knew something needed to be said to break it. "Might want to pull her back in, I'm rolling up the window." He nodded toward Socks. "She has the makings of a good truck dog."

Hannah didn't reply, but her tepid smile disagreed.

Gabe packed up the practice mannequins used in the evening's training. Even with his head bent, his attention was on the group of Amish men not far from the table where he was working. One of them was the man who'd been with Hannah at the restaurant. Gabe concentrated on ignoring the impulse to scrutinize the man, or eavesdrop on the conversation. He'd say this for the guy, he didn't say much, he'd been quick to be recertified and he had the obvious respect of the men in the community.

Two of the group broke off and approached the table. One of them Gabe recognized as the blond man who'd been at the pond. The other's similarity in looks suggested he was a relative.

His fellow rescuer greeted him with a nod. "I'd have felt a lot more confident if I'd have had this refresher *before* I had to use CPR the other day."

Gabe grinned at the young Amish man. "You did great, Gideon. I should've had you teaching the course."

"*Ja*, well, it helped that you were right there beside me at the pond. Helps also that you're able to teach these classes locally. Otherwise we'd have had to hire drivers and travel some distance to take the training."

"All part of my job now. I aim to do whatever I can. Who knows when it might save a life, right?"

"*Ach*, as long as Ben's the one who goes into the freezing water, I'm game. Now, if it was Samuel with me the other day, we'd still be debating about who went out on the ice."

The other blond man shook his head. "No, we wouldn't have. It would've been you. Being the older *bruder* has to count for something."

Gabe grinned at the siblings' interaction. Closing the lid on the mannequin case, he snapped it shut and looked up to see Samuel studying him.

"I'm also now older *bruder*, at least by a few months, to Hannah Lapp. I understand you were seen with her today. Is there anything that an older *bruder* needs to know about that?"

Gabe met his gaze. "The Amish grapevine works very quickly."

The man shrugged good-naturedly. "Almost as fast as the *Englisch*'s information highway."

"You probably already know that she found her dog then. That's all there was to it." *For now.* Call him foolish, but he hadn't given up yet. "I wish Hannah nothing but the best." *Which hopefully includes me in her life.*

Hannah's brother-in-law scrutinized him further before smiling slightly. "It was horses that got me. See you around."

Gabe shook his head as he watched the brothers

leave. He didn't have long to ponder the curious re-
mark when another Amish man approached the table.

With a grin, Gabe nodded at the newcomer. "Aaron.
It's good to see you. How've you been?" He'd met
Aaron Raber at a party when Gabe was taking classes
at the nearby junior college years ago. In his *rumspringa*, the Amish man had been one of the young
men in their run-around years that seemed to find
anything within horse-and-buggy—or for a few, even
car—range that remotely resembled a party. Aaron
was the one who'd invited Gabe to the gathering where
he'd met Hannah. He nodded to the short cast the man
was wearing on his arm. They'd worked around it in
order to complete his training. "You doing all right?"

"I'm *gut*. I see you found a way back into the area."

"Well, God opens doors. Although maybe sometimes it's windows."

"This isn't what I remember you doing when you
left. You were in some kind of...mechanics, *ja*?"

"Yeah, well. I had a change of heart. Went home to
Madison. Finished up there. Still mechanics of some
kind, I guess. Human body mechanics. Speaking of
which, is your brother the one that went in after the
boy?"

"That'd be Ben. Never hesitates to step up when
needed. *Gut* man to have in a pinch." The man quickly
moved on from his younger brother's heroics. "Were
there any classes for mechanics down in Madison?"

Obviously, the man wanted to draw the conversation back to his topic. Gabe didn't have a problem with
that. He nodded. "There are some good tech schools

in Madison. I hear it has one of the best diesel programs in the country."

The dark-haired Amish man leaned in from the opposite side of the table. "Any way of getting *gut* training without taking the classes?"

Gabe frowned as he considered the question. "In what way?"

"We don't use electricity from the grid, so the community gets its power from motors, both gasoline and diesel. From refrigerators in the home to huge machinery at the sawmill and Schrock Brothers' Furniture. Things are changing. Land's tight. Not as many opportunities to farm. Have to come up with other ways to make a living and support a family. Someone in the Plain community needs to be able to repair and sell all these motors, big and small. Why not me?"

The man had a point. And had found a potential niche into the community business environment. "I met a guy at school," Gabe said. "His dad has a repair shop in Madison where some of the students interned. He'd know more than I do. I can get you his number if you think it'll help."

At the man's enthusiastic nod, Gabe pulled out his phone and shuffled through his contacts. He looked over at Aaron. "You got a phone?"

Aaron pulled out a device and rattled off the number. "For the moment. Until I get baptized." He half smiled. "Followed shortly after by marriage."

Gabe wanted to be happy for the man, but the emotion that initially surfaced was envy instead. Keeping his expression neutral, he bent his head over his phone as he sent the contact information. "Congratulations."

"You might've met her. She was in the fabric shop the day Ruth Schrock became ill."

There might've been another woman in the shop that day. There also might've been a marching band in there. Gabe didn't remember anything about that day except his patient and seeing Hannah again. "Sweet girl. Again, congratulations."

"Denki." Aaron lifted up his phone and tipped it toward Gabe. "And *denki* for this. I appreciate it. I hope things work out for you, as well."

Gabe eyed him sharply, remembering the news that he and Hannah had been together had already raced around the community.

Aaron's eyebrows peaked at his pointed interest. "On your new job." Pocketing his phone, he waved and exited the fire department's meeting room. Although other men nearby, *Englisch* and Amish, nodded as they broke up their conversations and left, no one else approached Gabe as he finished packing up the abbreviated training mannequins and other supplies and loaded them in his truck.

So, Hannah and he were news around the community. As Gabe headed back to his apartment, he wondered what being the new hot topic on the Amish grapevine meant for his chances with the woman he loved.

Chapter Six

Hannah looked up from her needlework at Dash's sharp bark. Socks, curled up beside Hannah's chair, jumped to her feet. Emitting a soft whine, she trotted to the door. Across the room, Hannah's *daed* tipped down the corner of the newspaper he was reading to meet Hannah's frown. Paul, the only one of her four younger brothers currently at home, looked up from where he was whittling at the kitchen table.

A moment later, a series of furious barks had Hannah springing to her feet as well and hurrying to the door. Flinging it open, she stepped out onto the porch with Socks close beside her. Wrapping her arms about her to ward off the cold, Hannah searched the darkness for the male Border collie. Her hand rubbed Socks's silky head as her mind thought back to the dog's disappearance three days earlier and the frayed rope found on her.

Hannah's shoulders sagged in relief when she made out the white markings on the black-and-white dog as he zipped back and forth across the top of the lane.

"Here, Dash. Come here, boy," she called for him.

After a moment's hesitation, the dog loped to the house and leaped up onto the porch. With a soft growl, he positioned himself at the top of the steps, looking out.

"Everything all right?" Hannah turned to see her *daed* silhouetted in the doorway, the gas lamps from inside the house a soft glow behind him.

"I think so, *Daed*. I don't see anything."

Zebulun Lapp nodded and disappeared into the house. Calling to Dash, Hannah stepped closer to the door her *daed* had left open.

"Come here, boy. Why don't you come inside?" Although she sighed, Hannah wasn't surprised when the Border collie just turned his head to look at her before facing the darkness beyond the porch again. Dash had never liked it in the house. At most, he might enter and circle the room to ensure everything was as it should be before racing for the door again. Tonight, he remained braced at the edge of the porch. Hannah closed the door and crossed to him, wishing she had his enhanced senses, as she, too, stared into the night.

A dim light glowed where the road was. Then it was gone. Hannah blinked, trying to figure out what it might've been. It wasn't a flashlight beam. She hissed in a breath when it came to her. It'd been a dome light of an *Englisch* car. If that was so, why was it sitting on the dark road beyond the end of their lane? Holding her breath, she focused on listening. In the cold, still night, she made out the quiet rumble of a car engine. But no corresponding headlamps lit up the road. She tried once again to coax Dash inside with the same lack of success; instead, the dog kept looking toward the direction of the vehicle.

Kneeling beside him, Hannah wrapped her arms

around his taut shoulders. Socks huddled on her other side. Keeping one arm around Dash, Hannah looped the other around Socks, taking comfort from the contact of their warm, vibrant bodies. All three focused their attention on the road.

Dash stiffened, and Socks lifted her head at the faint sound of barking. Hannah narrowed her eyes on the muted glow in the distance of an *Englisch* neighbor's yard light. From numerous trips past, she knew a large black-and-brown dog roamed their yard. The trio on the porch listened as the barking continued, followed abruptly by the muffled sound of a human yelp. Unbidden, the image of the man who'd approached her and Socks on the sidewalk in town popped into her head. Chilled by the thought of the man, as well as the permeating cold, Hannah hugged her dogs more tightly. A roar of an engine cut through the night, this time with headlamps piercing the darkness. The lights headed in the direction of town.

Conscious now of the cold nipping at her nose and ears and seeping into the parts of her not in contact with the dogs, Hannah stood. With one last look toward disappearing lights, she and Socks returned to the house. Dash stayed planted on the porch.

It took an hour and a hot cup of tea for Hannah to settle down. Still, she poked herself with her needle when Dash barked again. It was a different bark from earlier, but Hannah was up and at the door before the dog's last yips concluded.

There was no questioning the clatter of hooves on the lane's frozen ground as a horse and buggy pulled up in the darkness.

"Malachi?" Hannah watched as an Amish man sprang out, foregoing the buggy's step in his urgency. There was no sign of her friend. Her fingers tightened on the doorknob. "Where's Ruth?"

Malachi was panting as if he'd run the distance between the two farms himself. He braced his hands on both sides of the door. "The *boppeli*!"

There was no need to say more. Hannah jerked her cloak and bonnet from the nearby pegs on the wall. Malachi anxiously looked behind her into the large open room. "Your *mamm*?"

"Not here. Paul!" she called to her younger *bruder*. "Run down to the phone shack and call the midwife. Tell her that Ruth Schrock is having her baby." Hannah was halfway across the yard before Malachi caught up with her. With a hand at her elbow, he assisted her into the buggy, almost tossing her across the seat in his excitement before scrambling in after her.

Hannah braced a hand on the buggy's dash as they swung out of the yard. "How is she?"

Malachi encouraged his gelding to pick up the pace. "She's bossy."

Bringing her hands to her lap, Hannah clasped them so tightly she felt the cut of her short nails on her skin. "That's her normal state. Obviously labor hasn't affected her much."

There was little further conversation as tension filled the buggy on the ride between the two farms. Hannah's heart raced with the cadence of the horse's quick beat on the road. Her friend needed help, but she'd never delivered a *boppeli* before. Her *mamm*, mother of several children, was visiting relatives in another district and wouldn't be home tonight. Rocking with the motion of the buggy, Hannah tried to concentrate on the upcoming event, but her ability to focus vaporized like the condensed air that drifted along the horse's black mane. They needed more help. *Please,* Gott, *let Paul reach the midwife. Please let her arrive soon.*

It seemed Malachi could hear her thoughts. "You ever done this before?"

The brisk air stung Hannah's nose as she drew in a shaky breath. She considered stretching her experience to comfort both herself and the dad-to-be, but the truth popped out instead. "I've helped *Daed* deliver several of our dairy calves."

Malachi was quiet for a moment before snorting. "Ruth's pragmatic, but I'll leave it to you to tell her you're comparing her delivery to that of a Holstein."

She recognized the humor for what it was, a defense against fear. A quick grab of the buggy's door frame kept her from swaying into Malachi as they swung into the lane before coming to a rocking stop in front of the house.

"You go on in. I need to take care of Kip. I'm… I'm hoping we don't need him the rest of the night."

Although she wanted to dash into the house, Hannah picked her way over the combination of frozen, rutted ground and smooth, icy puddles. When she reached the front door, a guarded woofing emanated from the other side. "It's okay, Rascal," she soothed. "It's me." Twisting the handle, Hannah stepped inside to be greeted by the Border collie Ruth had gotten from her as a puppy a year ago. Shooting a glance toward the door she knew led to a downstairs bedroom, Hannah bent to give the dog's head a brief rub. "I know. It's a pretty exciting night."

Her heart rate jumped at the continued lull from the room as she hastily shed her outer gear to hang it on the nearby pegs. She'd expected some type of greeting. Surely her friend had heard her come in? Hesitantly, Hannah crossed the large open room. "Ruth? Are you there?"

There were a few more beats of heavy silence as she approached the door before an exasperated "Just where did you think I'd be?" floated through the opening.

Hannah exhaled a breath she wasn't aware of holding. Her friend sounded more annoyed than distressed. "With you, it's hard to tell." She stepped into the room, glancing immediately toward the bed. Finding it empty, she blinked in surprise.

"*Ach*, it's a pretty safe guess tonight. Did you leave Malachi at your place?"

At her friend's comment, Hannah whirled to find Ruth across the lantern-lit room, pulling miniature clothing from a wooden chest. Shaking her head, she crossed to join her. "He'll be here in a moment. He's taking care of Kip. What are you doing up? From the way Malachi came racing to our house, I expected to find you…well, not up and around."

"There always seemed to be something to do, other than get these out." Ruth ran a finger down the dark blue material. "I made them months ago. But, after Louisa, I put them away. Just…just in case." She turned toward Hannah, a little gown and cap in her hands. Although she sounded nonchalant, her appearance told a different story. Auburn hair stuck in sweaty tendrils around her flushed face. Her green eyes were clear, but filled with relief at the sight of company. They shifted to the door, obviously searching to see if anyone else would be entering the room.

Hannah bit her lip. "I'm sorry. My *mamm* isn't home tonight. It's only me. Paul's calling for the midwife. I don't know when she'll be able to get here." She forced the reassuring smile she knew her friend needed to see onto her face. "I'm sure we'll be fine until then." Taking Ruth's arm, she steered her toward the bed. They were halfway across the room when Ruth gasped and hunched forward, crossing her arms over her belly. Hannah could only pray as tension gripped the elbow under her fingertips. *Please,* Gott, *let us be fine.*

They stayed rooted in the center of the room until Ruth visibly relaxed. Lifting her head, she squinted at Hannah. "*Gut* thing I always thought you had more sense and composure than any natural woman should have."

Even though she hadn't moved, Hannah felt like she'd run to the neighbors' farm and back in empathy with the physical struggle of the woman beside her. She couldn't take Ruth's pain for her, but she'd help her in any other way she could, even if it was just mild distraction. "Well, one of us needed it," Ruth snorted as they crept the rest of the way to the bed. Flipping back the sheets, Hannah helped the pregnant woman into a sitting position.

Sighing, Ruth leaned her head against the headboard. "If you would do one thing for me?"

"Anything," Hannah immediately agreed. She pulled the sheets up to tuck around Ruth's rounded lap.

"Make sure my *kapp* stays on, as I think I'll be doing a considerable amount of praying tonight."

"I've got it." Hannah straightened Ruth's prayer covering and secured the pins. She understood Ruth's concern. The *Biewel* stated a woman's head should be covered when praying. As it also said they should pray without ceasing, Amish women wore head coverings continuously. Knowing she'd be doing a considerable amount of praying over the next hours as well, Hannah confirmed her own *kapp* was well anchored after the jolting ride.

"And Hannah?" Ruth reached out and clasped her hand. Hannah tried not to wince at the strong grip squeezing her fingers. "If I scream, don't tell anyone. I have a reputation to keep."

"That's *hochmut*." Hannah surreptitiously wiggled her tingling fingers when Ruth released her hand.

"Believe me," Ruth groaned softly as she shifted. "Of the many things I'm feeling right now, pride is not one of them." She eyed Hannah with a frown. "We can't all be models of *demut* and *gelassenheit* like you."

Hannah's lips twitched as she adjusted pillows behind Ruth's back. "I won't tell," she promised. "Besides, no one would believe me if I did. They all figure if you make any sound at all, it'll be to give orders."

"*Ach*, they're right." Ruth settled back in obvious relief at the new position. For a few moments, the room was quiet as she gently massaged her belly. When she spoke, it was so soft that Hannah had to lean forward to hear her whispered words.

"So here's the first one. If anything happens to me, take care of my husband."

Hannah froze. Ruth looked up, and the two women shared a glance. Only clamping her tongue between her teeth kept Hannah from bursting into tears at her friend's obvious concern. They were both thinking of the loss of Louisa Weaver and her unborn baby. Careful not to jostle the other woman, Hannah sat on the side of the bed and took both of Ruth's unresisting hands in hers.

"Whatever happens will be according to *Gott*'s will. So we shouldn't worry about that. I'm thinking your worry should be more about the sleep you'll be missing when a beautiful *boppeli* keeps you up at nights. And you and Malachi will be *wunderbar* parents who'll give this child many siblings to play with in the future. Everything will be fine." Hannah pressed her lips together in a trembling smile. *Please, Gott, let me be right about that.*

With a final squeeze of her friend's hands, Hannah stood and made her way to the open door. Facing the living room, she spoke over her shoulder. She didn't want Ruth to see her face, as she was struggling to mask her own fears. "Now I have some things to get ready. I'll be back in a moment." Striding quickly into the kitchen, Hannah ensured she wasn't in the line of sight of the open bedroom door when she hugged herself and bowed her head. *Please, Gott, let me know what to do to help her. And please, please have the midwife hurry.* With a deep breath, she raised her head. Moving about Ruth's home, she gathered clean sheets, towels and rubbing alcohol while racking her brain for anything else that might be needed for the pending birth.

Chapter Seven

Gabe forked up another bite of meat loaf. He'd made a few lunches at his apartment—meaning he'd opened up a few cans of soup—but had been eating all his suppers at The Dew Drop. It wasn't that he was at a loss in a kitchen, but that the Dew was such a winner. And its warm, cheery atmosphere was much better than spending an evening at home. Alone. Thinking about a woman who wasn't likely to be sharing any home with him.

Among the clatter of silverware and quiet buzz of conversations, he heard the ringtone and vibration of a phone on a nearby table. Idly looking over, Gabe saw Martha Edigers, fellow Mennonite and the local midwife, frown as she put down her fork and picked up the device. The older woman must struggle with her hearing, as the volume was turned up loud enough for Gabe to hear from his own booth. He straightened abruptly at one of the names mentioned as Mrs. Edigers listened to the excited male voice on the phone. Gabe had his wallet out and was tossing a bill on the table by the time the woman disconnected the call. He slid out of the booth and was in front of Mrs. Ediger's table in time to see her gather up her coat and fill in her husband on the call.

"That was Paul Lapp. Ruth Schrock is having her baby. Hannah Lapp is with her, but I need to go now."

"Anything I can do to help?" Gabe nodded at the woman's husband before shifting his gaze back to the midwife. The gray-haired woman studied him with narrowed eyes for a moment.

"You know, I might need you. I usually have an assistant, but she's laid up following a foot surgery. I've heard you know what you're about. Does that include birthing babies?"

"Once. I was more anxious than the new parents. But I can bring along some equipment in case it's needed and add a hand if necessary." As Mr. Edigers made a move to rise, Gabe continued, "And I'd be happy to drive."

Mrs. Edigers covered her husband's hand with her own. "You finish your dinner. I'll see you at home. It's hard to tell on these first ones. I don't know when I'll be back." They shared a smile. It apparently was a common farewell for them. Reaching out a hand, Gabe assisted the midwife out of her chair and on with her coat.

"I need to grab some supplies before we head out."

"My truck's out front. Just tell me where we're going first."

After swinging by the midwife's house to pick up necessities, they were headed out of town minutes later. They'd reached the highway before Gabe felt a sting of chagrin for inviting himself along. Granted, it was always helpful to have medical assistance available for a home delivery. From what he'd heard, though, the older woman seated beside him had been successfully delivering babies in Miller's Creek for as long as anyone could remember. But once he'd heard Hannah's name, Gabe acknowledged it would've been difficult to dissuade him from offering assistance, just for the chance to see her and ensure she was all right.

Squirming with embarrassment, he glanced over at his passenger. "I appreciate you letting me come along."

Mrs. Edigers smiled benignly. "Glad to have your help. You never know in these situations." Her smile ebbed. "The community's somewhat tense after a recent loss."

"I'd heard about that."

"The Amish don't carry health insurance. When someone has bills to cover, they rally around with fundraisers. But they try to keep costs down. For them, childbirth is natural and quite common. That's why many of the women don't seek medical help until later in the pregnancy. Sometimes things that could be caught and prevented, aren't." She shook her head. "Things like eclampsia."

Gabe had heard something to that effect. The complication could be fatal to mother and child.

Mrs. Edigers sighed. "Some women go to chiropractors, asking for help on pregnancies. I don't know why they're more comfortable going there than other medical facilities. I help where I can. Over the years, I've gained a level of trust. It would be wonderful, though, if someone from their community would become a midwife."

"How is that possible? They stop school after eighth grade."

"There are certifications that can be earned through apprenticeships. Wisconsin currently recognizes them." She directed his turn onto a country road. "You know the Schrocks?"

"Met them." Gabe couldn't recall if introductions had been done that day in the fabric shop. Beyond his patient's needs, all he'd seen and known that day was Hannah. But he'd remembered Ruth from before. "Briefly. I…um…am more acquainted with Hannah Lapp."

From the weight of the gaze he felt across the truck's cab, Gabe figured the Amish information highway must have tracks through the midwife's office. Mrs. Edigers didn't comment, but a quick glance in her direction revealed an enigmatic smile. "I'm sure everything will work out fine."

With Mrs. Edigers's directions and Gabe's heavy foot on the pedal, they were soon pulling in front of a large white farmhouse. In the moment before he shut off the truck, the headlights revealed a man stepping out onto the porch, a black-and-white dog at his side. Gabe gathered equipment from his side of the cab and hurried around to help the midwife over the rough, frozen yard. Woofing once to let them know he knew they were there, the Border collie stayed beside the man, his white-tipped tail waving gently over his back.

Geared to respond to any medical or emergency situation, Gabe blew out a few breaths to remind himself it wasn't him who'd been called out to the farm. He was self-invited backup. Keeping a hand under the older woman's elbow, he assisted her up the stairs.

"Hello, Malachi. How's she doing?"

The blond man looked like he wasn't sure how to answer the question. *"Gut?"*

Mrs. Edigers patted his arm. "Don't get too comfortable out here. Even if Ruth isn't looking for you again soon, I will be to have you help catch the baby."

The man's broad shoulders rose and fell in a shaky sigh. With a smile, the midwife patted his arm again and disappeared into the house.

Turning to Gabe, Malachi reached out a hand. *"Denki* for bringing her out." Raising an eyebrow at the unusual action for an Amish man, Gabe shifted the bag of equipment to his other hand and shook it. It was surely an unusual evening for the pending father.

"You Samuel and Gideon's brother?" It was a logical assumption. There was a family resemblance to the two men who'd been at the fire department training session. Gideon had said the day of the cold water rescue that he worked at the furniture business in town. The only one Gabe had seen so far was called Schrock Brothers. But in Amish communities, where certain surnames were very common, there could be ten different Schrock families.

"Depends on if they were behaving."

Gabe grinned and reached down to acquaint himself with the dog before running his hand over its smooth head. "Very much so. I saw them at a CPR training session last night and met Gideon when he and Ben Raber rescued the boy at the pond."

"Then I guess I'll claim them." Malachi looked over his shoulder through the door into the house. "I…ah… need to go back inside." The man twisted his work-hardened hands together. Gabe read both apprehension and eagerness in the gesture.

"Absolutely." Gabe quickly crossed the porch. Malachi followed, looking immediately to a closed door across the large, simply furnished room once they stepped inside the house.

He closed the outer door with a quiet click. "Actually, it was *gut* to step away for a moment. It's hard to see her in… She isn't saying much of anything." Malachi's smile was wry, but his eyes remained solemn. "Which is abnormal for Ruth." He exhaled in a long stream through pursed lips. "I feel…helpless. I'm so glad Hannah came earlier. She's been a comfort to Ruth."

Gabe gripped the man's shoulder and squeezed it gently. Even though she wasn't and may never be his, the thought of Hannah someday bringing his child into the world swept him with empathy for this obviously strong man who felt powerless in the face of his wife's pain. "I'm sure you are a great comfort to Ruth, as well."

Malachi swallowed and nodded. "I'm going to go back in. Help yourself to anything you want in the kitchen." He glanced toward the dog. "All I can offer is Rascal for company while you wait."

"We'll be fine." Releasing his grip, Gabe glanced down at the dog. Relieving Gabe of the supplies with a final nod, Malachi crossed to the closed door, his tread slow on the linoleum floor. Pausing in front of it, he took a deep breath, turned the handle, stepped decisively into the quiet room and closed the door behind him.

The Border collie looked toward the door and whined softly. Gabe knelt to give him a few reassuring pats. "They'll be fine, as well." Rising to his feet, he wandered briefly around the room before stopping in front of an oak rocker. Marveling at the workmanship, he decided it was too small for him and settled into the upholstered mission-style chair nearby. Shifting through a stack of *Budgets*, he began flipping through the Amish newspaper by the illumination of a nearby gas light. The dog lay down between the two chairs, chin on paws, to face the bedroom door. The room was quiet except for the ticking of the nearby wall clock and the soft rustle of turning pages.

Fifteen minutes later, both man and dog started when a strident tone intruded in the silence. It took Gabe a moment to process that his pager was going off in the room otherwise void of electronics. Hushing the device, he quickly contacted dispatch. A moment later, he rapped softly on the closed bedroom door.

When Hannah cracked the door open, he smiled in relief at the composure on her face. "How are things going?"

"*Gut*. We're still waiting. The *boppeli* is being a little shy."

"I need to go on a call. I don't know how long I'll be gone. Will that be an issue for Mrs. Edigers?"

Hannah turned back toward the unseen room. Following a short, murmured discussion, she shook her head. "*Nee*. She's expecting to be here a *gut* while yet."

Gabe nodded. "Okay. I'll see you later." Although he wished for a more lingering farewell, he needed to get going. Giving another abrupt nod, he headed for the door.

That Hannah was still watching him when he'd looked back while closing it prompted an extra zip in his step as Gabe hustled across the frozen ground to his truck.

The flashing blue light on his vehicle reflected over the snowy landscape as he retraced his way toward Miller's Creek. Gabe recognized the address. On the distant outskirts of town, he swung into a driveway, the truck shuddering as it slid into the frozen ruts in the unplowed surface. Abandoned vehicles lined the lane to a dilapidated house and machine shed. The sign above the wide shed door was shattered on the left side, leaving only the word REPAIR visible, like it was making a plea instead of advertising a business.

A dim glow, generating from a bare bulb in a simple white socket, lit the porch. Gear in hand, Gabe headed for the ragged door beyond. He'd heard of this guy. Clay Weathers had been a respected local mechanic until a snowmobile accident a few years ago. He'd eventually recovered from his back injury. He hadn't recovered from the pain medications he'd become addicted to during the process. His business, health, friends and family had been left behind in the wake of the hold opioids now had on him.

Gabe brushed his pocket to confirm he had naloxone as he trod across the weathered porch. The call had been for a deep laceration but, given the story on the man, other issues were possible. Rapping firmly on the warped screen door, he loudly announced himself. Gabe was about to try the handle when a muffled "Come in" filtered through the door.

Pushing it open, Gabe stepped into a small, shabby living room to find who he presumed to be his patient, sitting in a worn recliner with the footrest extended. A bloody towel was wrapped around the man's hand. The man's left calf was bare except for the blood-stained towel pressed to it with his free hand. A few more similarly soiled towels lay beside the chair.

"Looks like you tangled with something." Upon setting down his gear, Gabe donned his personal protective equipment and leaned over the man. He nodded to the man's leg. "May I?"

Wearily nodding, the man pulled his hand back. Gabe examined the leg. Through the smeared blood, he could see some gashes and a seeping puncture wound. "Dog bite?" he confirmed.

"Yup, but he didn't mean it. Was my fault. I startled him."

Placing clean gauze on the puncture wound, Gabe directed the man to place pressure against it. "Let's get that bleeding stopped before we clean you up." Turning his attention to the man's hand, Gabe unwrapped the soiled towel to find similar wounds, although these were no longer bleeding. "Do you know the dog? Is this normal behavior for it? Do you know if it's up-to-date on its rabies shots?"

"No, no. He's a good dog. He's in good shape."

Gabe frowned. He didn't know if he was talking more to Clay Weathers or to what the man was under the influence of. Gathering what he needed, Gabe began cleaning and treating the man's hand.

"When was the last time you had a tetanus shot?"

Now the man frowned. His eyes, even with their constricted pupils, looked melancholy. "I used to keep up with that. Because of the shop. I… I've had one."

"Do you want to go to the hospital? I don't think these will require stitches, but I recommend having them checked out, as dog bites are prone to infection." He couldn't make the man go to the hospital. And the choice not to go affected what Gabe could do for him. But if he went, perhaps Clay Weathers would allow the hospital to assist him with other issues.

"Nah. I'll be all right." The man's head dropped to the worn headrest of the recliner, and he closed his eyes.

Gabe sighed as he wrapped gauze around the man's hand. "You'll need to continue to clean the wounds and put antibiotic ointment on them." Finishing with the hand, Gabe turned his attention to the leg to find the bleeding had stopped. "I highly recommend seeking out your personal physician for future care, especially if it gets infected."

Attending to the man's calf, Gabe felt rather than saw the man's shrug. He wasn't surprised with the reaction. It was what he'd expected. The man had his reasons not to want to see a health official. Still, the situation saddened Gabe.

After doing all he could to ensure Clay Weathers had the best possible chance he could give him for healthy recovery, Gabe packed up his gear to go. Stopping at the door, he turned back toward the man. "I can't emphasize enough that you follow up with your doctor."

"I'll be fine. I sure do thank you for your help. I got a little concerned when the bleeding wouldn't stop."

Gabe nodded in acknowledgment. He met the man's listless gaze across the small room. "I hope you seek out help, sir."

Clay lifted his unbandaged hand and waved. Lips

pressed in a firm line, Gabe stepped out the door and closed it behind him. His spirits only lifted when he got to the truck and remembered he was returning to Hannah.

Hannah stepped through the bedroom door and closed it softly behind her. Heading across the large open living area, she froze, wide-eyed, at the sight of Gabe, reading in the dim light of the gaslight, Rascal lying beside him on a braided rug.

"You're back."

Gabe rose from the chair. "How are things going?"

Emotions still high from recent events, Hannah had trouble finding her tongue. "*Gut*. Really *gut*. Everyone is doing fine." Her heart swelled. If things had been different, it might have been her in the adjoining room, with Gabe supporting and encouraging her through the delivery of their child. If she had met him that night, this might've been their second child.

Without thinking, she found herself moving across the room toward Gabe, unable to contain the wide smile that spread over her face. "The *boppeli* just arrived. A beautiful baby girl. New *mamm* and *daed* are getting acquainted with her." As if on cue, the sound of a newborn's cry penetrated the room.

"From the sound of it, she takes after her mother?" Gabe wore a teasing grin as he glanced at the closed bedroom door.

"*Ach*, that's unfair. Ruth was as quiet as a mouse all through delivery."

"I've heard that about Amish women." He shook his head. "I don't know how they do it."

"Neither do I." Hannah shared his smile. The volume of the cries increased. Although reluctant to break eye contact, Hannah turned toward the bathroom. "I have to gather some things and return." Gabe followed her across the room, the dog at his heels. Rummaging in a cupboard, she slid him a shy glance. "I'm glad you're back." Hannah blushed when she realized she'd verbalized her thought, hoping the murmur was low enough that Gabe hadn't heard it.

She caught her breath when he gently touched her elbow. "So am I." His hand slid down her arm to tangle with her fingers. "Do you ever think…?"

Yes. She did. Way too frequently recently. Hannah studied the floor. "I shouldn't."

Goosebumps rose on her forearms at the realization they'd both been thinking the same thing. She turned to look at this man who might have been her husband. Beyond his dear face, she saw the room behind him.

The contrast was blatant. Gabe's light brown hair wasn't in a bowl style, but curled closely to his head. There was no beard on his chin, a length determined by their years of marriage. If she'd been married to Gabe, the house where they lived wouldn't have a room lit with gas and lantern light. It probably wouldn't have a gas-powered refrigerator. There wouldn't be a few buggy and draft horses in the barn. But most critical of all, it wouldn't be with the support of the Amish community that would gather around, visiting the new *boppeli*. To support her, the new mother.

Because of the new father.

Which one did she want more? Which could she more easily live without? Right now, flush with the miracle of new life, and after witnessing the wonder of two awestruck parents holding their newborn, with her hand clasped in Gabe's warm, strong grip, and his green eyes soft on hers, Hannah knew if he would ask what she thought he'd wanted to ask years ago, she'd say yes.

Her eyes must have mirrored her confusion, as Gabe leaned closer, his other hand lifting to gently cup the back of her neck under her *kapp*. Eyelids fluttering down, Hannah swayed toward him.

Only to jerk back when the dog at their side yipped excitedly and trotted toward the bedroom door. Hastily dropping Gabe's hand, Hannah stepped away from him. Turning back to the cupboard, she stared into its depth a moment before she could recall what she was supposed to gather. When the bedroom door swung open a short while later, she was halfway across the room with her arms full of towels and other items.

Malachi stuck his head out the door. "Did you find everything you needed?"

"Ja." Hannah nodded, slipping past him into the room.

"I'm a *daed*," she heard Malachi announce to Gabe with some amazement.

Gabe's soft "Congratulations" followed them into the room before Malachi closed the door behind them.

Ruth was sitting up in bed, holding the baby, a captivated smile on her weary face as she looked down at her newborn daughter. Malachi crossed to the pair. Carefully setting a hip on the bed, he slid his arm about Ruth's shoulders.

"I'm glad it's a *dochder*," he murmured.

"Really?" Ruth's smile widened as she leaned against her husband.

"Really," he echoed. "I hope she's just like you."

Ruth turned her head toward Malachi. This time her tone was heavy with skepticism. "Really?"

"*Ja*. The world needs people like you." Dipping his head, he kissed her nose. "Just not too many of them."

Hannah busied herself on the other side of the room, her emotions warring between yearning and mild embarrassment at having witnessed the tender exchange.

She was so, so happy for her friend. Sliding another glance at the trio on the bed, Hannah bit her tongue when a sliver of envy slipped in to dilute her joy. Quickly, she quashed the errant feeling as she assisted Mrs. Edigers in tidying up the room. Still, she conceded, as she sniffed back a few tears, a family would be *wunderbar*. She yearned to be a mother. Gabe would be a tender father. If only…

When Mrs. Edigers instructed Gabe to take Hannah home some time later, despite her exhaustion, Hannah was reluctant to go. What had begun with anxiety had ended with awe.

Before they left, Gabe accepted Malachi's offer to hold his daughter, Deborah. Hannah's breath had caught at seeing the tiny infant in his strong arms. She'd turned away, but not before Ruth noticed Hannah's expression and raised her eyebrows almost to her hairline.

If the ride over had seemed endless, the return trip was too short. They didn't talk, but by tacit agreement, held hands over the front seat's console. Gabe helped her out of the truck and walked her to the door, fingers again entwined. Although it was still a few hours until sunrise, Hannah was conscious that any minute her parents might be rising to prepare for chores. Still, she tightened her grip and didn't resist when Gabe used their grasp to swing her around and take her other hand.

"That could've been us, you know." His breath in the cold morning air wafted away an inch from her face.

"Ja," she whispered.

"It still could."

Hannah didn't say anything. She couldn't. She was breathless. Maybe it was the wonder of the night, but anything seemed possible at the moment. Even marrying the man she'd fallen in love with years ago.

Gabe tugged gently on her fingers, and she eased forward. The warm air of his breath caressed her cheek as he leaned closer.

A light flicked on in her parent's bedroom. She immediately took a step back. In the light of the now-shadowed porch, she saw Gabe's eyes as he sighed ruefully.

With a subdued smile on her face, Hannah dropped his hands. "Good night."

"Good night," he echoed, mirroring her expression. Walking back to the truck, Gabe gave her a last look before getting in.

In his eyes, she'd seen hope. And a promise.

Hope for them? A promise for their future? Hannah knew what she hoped for and the future she was beginning to acknowledge she wanted, but it needed to be *Gott*'s will, not hers. Knowing she wouldn't sleep the rest of the night, Hannah quietly made her way into the house.

Chapter Eight

"Yes, I understand." Although he didn't. Gabe's hand tightened around the phone. "No, I appreciate you calling. I'd much rather hear it direct than from another source. Okay. I'll… I'll work with that. Sure. Thanks. I appreciate it. Bye." Gabe slowly lowered the phone. There was no need for him to disconnect the call. The caller, obviously relieved to have finished the conversation, had hung up almost before Gabe's distracted farewell. Gabe couldn't blame her. Most people didn't like being the bearer of bad news.

The grant for his position had fallen through. No grant, no funding. No funding, no job. No job, no reason for him to be here. No reason for him to be here, no chance to build a future with Hannah.

Tucking the phone back into his pocket, Gabe chided himself for thinking of the situation only from his perspective. He'd been brought in as a paid employee to assist the local volunteer fire department with EMS needs. The local department was very good, but with more residents working outside of the district, along with other factors, the number of volunteers had decreased. As over fifty percent of service calls were for EMS, Gabe's involvement greatly reduced the stress on the diminished squad. Due to his training, he could also provide more advanced emergency care. Miller's Creek would be affected by the loss of Gabe's contributions to the community. The emergency needs of the area were more important than his personal issues.

Gabe wanted to be completely altruistic, but the progress he'd been making with a local EMS service wasn't running through his mind as he stared across the apartment he'd finally finished moving into. *We've come so far. Last night at the Schrocks', I know she felt what I felt. That we could have something precious and rare.*

Now the only things precious and rare were the few days he had left in Miller's Creek. He was going to be paid through the end of the month. The administrator had assured him they'd apply for another grant, but it might take months before it went through. And although he was a careful money manager, he wasn't in a position to go without a job. Gabe shoved himself up from the couch. He shouldn't be surprised. Halfway through the interview process, the administration that'd hired him had become evasive with some of his questions. But he'd been so thrilled to find a job in Miller's Creek he hadn't noticed their ambiguity. When he'd been advised to report to someone else before he'd even moved into the area, he'd shrugged it off, more focused on the challenge of setting up the program than caring who his supervisor was.

Gabe stalked to the window, seeing not the view outside it, but the blue curtains that surrounded the wooden frame. Well, he had a few weeks left. A few weeks to complete the training he'd already started. Reaching out, he slid a finger down the fabric. A few short weeks to convince the woman he'd never stopped loving that he was worth all she'd have to give up to be with him.

The bolt of fabric dropped with a thud to the floor. Cindy Borders and the other *Englisch* customer who'd been talking at the counter looked over to Hannah at the sound.

"Are you all right?"

"Ja," Hannah mumbled, hastening to pick up the dark green material and set it on the counter. "It slipped through my fingers."

As Gabe was going to, if what the women were discussing was true.

"The grant fell through? We're losing our new EMS service?" She swallowed as she unrolled material from the bolt to stretch it across the ruler embedded in the counter's surface. Would there be any reason for Gabe to stay in the area if the grant was lost?

"Yes. A shame, isn't it? We were so excited for the town to have a program established. Even if they leave right away from a neighboring area, it still takes extra time to arrive. And when the weather gets bad out, it takes even longer." The *Englisch* woman who'd found Hannah's dog shook her head.

The other woman nodded. "Hate to think of what would've happened to the Winston boy without the young man that's been working in the area." She smiled at Hannah. "And of course, the Amish men that pulled him from the pond."

"A yard and a half of this fabric?" Hannah gave her a small smile in return. She picked up the scissors, her thoughts not on the green material, but on the young man just mentioned.

"Yes, please." Mrs. Borders sighed. "Too bad the whole community won't do something like the Amish do." Cocking her head, she regarded Hannah. "Don't you do different types of fundraisers to help cover medical costs and other things for your members? If I recall correctly, there was a whole slew of events before the Amish school was built some years back. And what is it I read about in some Amish communities?" Her forehead furrowed like a freshly plowed field. "Mud sales?"

It was true. Hannah recalled the numerous bake sales, pancake breakfasts and BBQ dinners held to raise money for the local teacher's salary and other school expenses. A mud sale, an auction usually held in the spring when the footing was soggy, hence the name, was a traditional way some Amish districts raised money for their volunteer fire departments.

"Ja." Folding the now-cut material and setting the rewrapped bolt on the table behind her, she reached for the next color in the stack. "How much of this one?"

"Half a yard. Hopefully it will look like it's supposed to when I'm done. I don't have near the talent displayed in your shop." Mrs. Borders's attention rested on the quilt hung on the wall behind where Hannah worked, before straying to the others that decorated the borders of the room. "These are so beautiful. If something like a quilt auction were held, I'd be sitting in the front row, spending much more than my husband would like." She gently elbowed the woman beside her. "Or knows about."

"I tell mine it's worth it as they serve a dual purpose. It's a feast for the eyes and warmth for the toes. And I don't complain about the money he spends on fishing gear."

Mrs. Borders smiled conspiratorially. "Just think of the money an auction selling both could raise. With something like that, we might not even need a grant in order to keep the EMS service."

The women's conversation drifted to other topics as they paid for their purchases and left the store, but Hannah's thoughts lingered on what they'd said. While restocking the fabric bolts, her eyes drifted around the shop as the woman's had earlier, touching on each quilt. She had a good idea of what the *Englisch* would pay for a quilt. Amish, too, if the occasion was right. Would they see saving the EMS service for the community at large as a worthwhile cause? Her gaze lifted from the walls to the ceiling overhead. If they determined it was, could it happen in time to keep Gabe from leaving?

Winding her way through the rows back to the counter, Hannah pondered who she knew had recently completed quilts or nearly finished works-in-progress. And wondered if they could be convinced to part with them.

It might not be possible. But, as her employer had

said, much is lost for want of asking. Hannah knew just the place to start. If she had the courage.

Although her eyes were on the scrolling stitch in front of her, Hannah's ears were tuned to the chatter about the room. A considerable portion of the female Amish community, among them her *mamm* and younger *schweschder*, bordered the quilt frame stretched across the large room. Little girls in *kapps* and dresses played beneath its surface, including her niece, Lily. Hannah could hear the girl's infectious giggle drift up from under the center of the friendship star design.

Outwardly calm in appearance, Hannah's heart was beating so fast her hand trembled, making it a struggle to keep her normally precise stitches even. Since she'd heard the news yesterday about the grant, she'd known something needed to be done about the situation. Someone needed to step up. If not, the community would lose a resource that had already proven valuable. And she'd lose… Hannah glanced at the faces of the women lined along the borders of the quilt. Faces of women her age and older. Women she'd been raised to respect. A lifestyle she'd been raised to respect. A lifestyle in which she'd never caused a ripple.

Bowing her head to the fabric in front of her again, Hannah pressed her lips together. *This isn't about me. It's about what's best for the community. Who knows who might need emergency care at some critical time? Someone should do something.*

Her thread broke with a quiet pop. Leaning back from the framed material, Hannah wondered if maybe that was a *gut* thing, as her stitches today were lopsided and inconsistent. She flinched imperceptibly when a young girl instantly appeared beside her and handed her another threaded needle. Too old to play under the quilt and too young to take her place along its edge, the girl was one of a handful who contributed to quilting by threading needles for the older women while they sewed. Taking the needle, Hannah smiled at the earnest young face. It was a good thing the girl had threaded it because her own hands were shaking so much she couldn't have found the eye were it the size of a hay-mow door. *Someone needs to do something. I need to do something.*

But doing so meant making waves when she never had before.

Drawing in a shaky breath, she also drew a puzzled look from the young girl beside her. Hannah dropped her gaze to the thin pointed metal pinched between their fingers. The most elaborate quilt couldn't come together without the simple act of threading a needle. Not a big step, but one that had to happen in order for bigger things to come together. To save the extended emergency service program, and keep Gabe in the area, a first step needed to be taken. Could she thread that needle?

Much is lost for want of asking.

Her throat felt like it was coated with church spread. Hannah cleared it. When the voices around the room dropped one by one, she looked up to find herself the center of attention. Her thimbled finger clattered against the quilt frame. She took strength from Socks's warm weight, where the collie lay against her ankles.

Reaching forward with the newly threaded needle,

Hannah pushed it into the fabric. "I was talking with Ben Raber the other day. Asked him if he'd warmed up yet from going into the pond after the *Englisch* boy. He said he'd only recently stopped shivering." Hannah knew she'd have to rip out any stitches she was inflicting on the quilt in front of her, but she continued poking her needle through the fabric. "He said he'd heard the boy had made a complete recovery, thanks be to *Gott*. It amazed him, because when he pulled the boy out, there was no sign of life. *Gut* thing we had emergency service close."

"The *Englisch* need to take care of their own." The mutter came from the far end of the quilt. Although her attention remained unseeing on the quilt before her, Hannah took a deep breath and pitched her voice a little higher. "It could've easily been an Amish boy that went in. I know my *brieder* have skated on that pond before. It seems the ice wasn't the only thing that broke through. I heard the grant supporting local EMS did, as well. It would be a shame to lose the service now when we know it can save lives."

Murmurs rose from around the room. Due to the general buzz, Hannah couldn't tell if the comments were pro or con. She closed her eyes. An ally would be *wunderbar* about now. If only Ruth had been here, she wouldn't have hesitated to speak up. But her friend was still at home, getting acquainted with her new *dochder*. Hannah stabbed her finger with the needle when a voice cut through the murmurs.

"Samuel said it's a real benefit having someone local teach the required training needed for volunteer firefighters. It saves the men time when taking the classes. Before, they had to hire drivers to take them out of the county. Classes are more economical, too, with a local trainer."

Hannah glanced up to see her sister's impish smile. Gail's comment had been both sly and convincing. Amish women loved nothing more than a bargain.

Comments flowed around the room like creeks after a spring thaw.

"Well, there's no money for it now."

"Since when has the current lack of funds stopped a Plain community from doing what was needed? Didn't we raise money to expand the school?"

"We all know how dangerous farmwork can be. Faster arrival from local care could save a life, or a limb." The voice was elderly and tinged with experience.

For a moment, the only sounds in the room were the giggles and murmurs from the children under the quilt. All the women at its edges knew a friend or relative who'd been affected by some type of farming accident.

"What type of fundraiser are you thinking?"

As Hannah opened her mouth to respond, another voice forestalled her.

"You just want to keep this particular man here." Even the chatter under the quilt faded as Ruby Weaver's voice cut through the room. All faces turned toward the bishop's wife. Some with agreeing nods and sharp looks back toward Hannah. Concentrating on keeping a flush from rising in her cheeks, Hannah glanced around the quilt's border, searching for friendly faces before she faced the pale blue eyes on the far end of the patterned material. She was surprised at the number of frowning expressions she saw. Frowning at whom? Her or the bishop's wife? When Gail's was one of them, Hannah grasped a sliver of hope that they weren't all directed at her.

"I don't care who provides the service, I just think there will be times we wished we had it, and in those times it'll be too late for whoever is affected." Hannah knew she spoke the truth. But would she be willing to push past her reluctance to cause ripples in the community if Gabe wasn't involved?

"I'll ask again," prompted a voice across the room. "What type of fundraiser do you propose?"

Hannah could feel her pulse beating at the sides of her throat. She swallowed. "Well, many communities do mud sales to support their volunteer fire departments. This is something of an extension of that. So I was thinking we could arrange one for Miller's Creek."

"Does that mean you're going to organize it?" From Ruby, it sounded like an accusation.

Hannah's stomach hollowed at the question. It wasn't reluctance to tackle the amount of work in the project that flashed through her. But she'd already stepped out of her comfort zone. The tight-lipped woman across the quilt's friendship star design was probably going to be her future mother-in-law. One who was already unhappy with her. Should Hannah cause even more discord? She recalled how Ruby Weaver had been instrumental in driving Gail from the community. Not just once, but nearly again.

Should she continue on this path? This project idea was more Hannah's will than the will of the community. Hannah had always obeyed what was best for the district. She darted a glance toward her *mamm*, working beside Gail on the opposite end of the quilt. Willa Lapp met her gaze with a small smile. Hannah relaxed. She glanced down at her hands, poised above the fabric. Fabric that wasn't useful if it remained on a bolt. Unless someone began working with it, it couldn't fulfill its purpose. What if it was *Gott*'s will that she do this? Just because it was what she wanted, did that mean it wasn't His wish, as well? Had He put the two *Englisch* women in the shop to talk about the topic?

The attention in the room was all on her. Hannah quickly searched for any nudging of self-will and found a snippet of peace instead.

She nodded. "*Ja*. I am. I propose we hold an auction. Any objections if we start with this quilt? I'm sure that Barbara at the shop would donate to the cause, as well. What else can we provide to raise money for this project?" She made eye contact with each woman around the room, although it was difficult to hold Ruby Weaver's stony gaze. "And I'm counting on you to bring other items, as well."

Hannah released Daisy from where the mare had been tied to the post. She'd done it. And she'd survived. After some initial reluctance, and with furtive glances toward the bishop's wife after every positive comment, an excited buzz had generated regarding the project.

"We'll show the *Englisch* how a fundraiser is done." Hannah had overheard the comments of a gray-haired stitcher a few seats down the quilt's border.

"Hush now, Waneta. That's *hochmut*," her neighbor had chided, but it'd been said with a conspirator's smile.

The project was launched. Now she had much work ahead to manage a successful execution.

Hannah's mouth was tired from the effort of keeping a smile on it for the past few hours. An initial grin had risen from the ladies growing enthusiasm, but she'd had to prop it up several times to encourage and persuade participants. And wear it as armor against Ruby Weaver's undisguised disapproval. When it was finally time to wrap up for the day, after polite goodbyes, Hannah had been one of the first out the door.

She felt guilty for wanting to escape. Although they'd come together, her *mamm* was catching a ride home with a neighbor while Hannah went into town to grab some groceries from the Bent 'N Dent. Hannah was looking forward to a few moments alone, except for Daisy and the *clip-clop* of her hooves on the road, to gather her thoughts.

Sighing, she stroked a hand down the mare's wintercoated neck. Had she done the right thing? She'd always striven to abandon her will for *Gott*'s. Was this His? Or hers? While some of the women had smiled benevolently as she'd left, assuming her motives were altruistic for the community, Hannah knew better. Trailing a hand along Daisy's side as she walked back to the buggy, she winced. Ruby Weaver had been right. Hannah wouldn't have even thought to raise funds if Gabe hadn't been involved.

"Well, sister. It's not like you to make waves. I always thought that was my role." At the sound of Gail's voice, Hannah turned to see her sister approaching, hand in

Dear Reader,

I am writing to announce the launch of a huge **FREE BOOKS GIVEAWAY**... and to let you know that YOU are entitled to choose up to FOUR fantastic books that WE pay for.

Try **Love Inspired® Romance Larger-Print** books and fall in love with inspirational romances that take you on an uplifting journey of faith, forgiveness and hope.

Try **Love Inspired® Suspense Larger-Print** books where courage and optimism unite in stories of faith and love in the face of danger.

Or TRY BOTH!

In return, we ask just one favor: Would you please participate in our brief Reader Survey? We'd love to hear from you.

This FREE BOOKS GIVEAWAY means that we pay for *everything!* We'll even cover the shipping, and no purchase is necessary, now or later. So please return your survey today. You'll get **Two Free Books** and **Two Mystery Gifts** from each series to try, altogether worth over **$20!**

Sincerely

Pam Powers

Pam Powers
For Harlequin Reader Service

Complete the survey below and return it today to receive up to 4 FREE BOOKS and FREE GIFTS guaranteed!

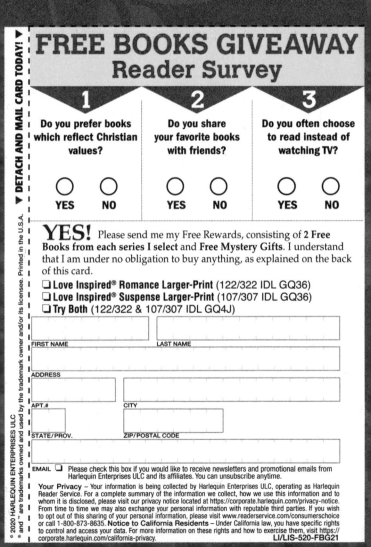

▼ DETACH AND MAIL CARD TODAY! ▼

FREE BOOKS GIVEAWAY
Reader Survey

1

Do you prefer books which reflect Christian values?

○ YES   ○ NO

2

Do you share your favorite books with friends?

○ YES   ○ NO

3

Do you often choose to read instead of watching TV?

○ YES   ○ NO

YES! Please send me my Free Rewards, consisting of **2 Free Books from each series I select** and **Free Mystery Gifts**. I understand that I am under no obligation to buy anything, as explained on the back of this card.

❏ Love Inspired® Romance Larger-Print (122/322 IDL GQ36)
❏ Love Inspired® Suspense Larger-Print (107/307 IDL GQ36)
❏ Try Both (122/322 & 107/307 IDL GQ4J)

FIRST NAME

LAST NAME

ADDRESS

APT.#

CITY

STATE/PROV.

ZIP/POSTAL CODE

EMAIL ❏ Please check this box if you would like to receive newsletters and promotional emails from Harlequin Enterprises ULC and its affiliates. You can unsubscribe anytime.

Your Privacy – Your information is being collected by Harlequin Enterprises ULC, operating as Harlequin Reader Service. For a complete summary of the information we collect, how we use this information and to whom it is disclosed, please visit our privacy notice located at https://corporate.harlequin.com/privacy-notice. From time to time we may also exchange your personal information with reputable third parties. If you wish to opt out of this sharing of your personal information, please visit www.readerservice.com/consumerschoice or call 1-800-873-8635. **Notice to California Residents** – Under California law, you have specific rights to control and access your data. For more information on these rights and how to exercise them, visit https://corporate.harlequin.com/california-privacy.

LI/LIS-520-FBG21

© 2020 HARLEQUIN ENTERPRISES ULC
® and ™ are trademarks owned and used by the trademark owner and/or its licensee. Printed in the U.S.A.

hand with a skipping Lily. "You were more of a 'one who rows the boat seldom has time to rock it' type."

Hannah smiled at the old Amish saying. "Maybe I learned from you."

"*Ach*, forgive me for that. But if that's the case, you handle it with much more grace than I ever did."

Hannah knelt to smooth her niece's *kapp* over the little girl's blond hair. "What's the saying about honey versus vinegar?"

"I don't think it's flies you want to catch. I think it's a handsome Mennonite man I've seen around town."

Straightening so quickly that Daisy jerked her head at the abrupt motion, Hannah shot her sister a quelling look. "Where did you get that idea?"

Gail snorted as she attended to her own horse, tied along the fence beside Daisy. "Your current romances, and the fact that you are finally having them, are the talk of the district." She paused, slanting a glance toward Lily, who'd bent to pet the patiently waiting Socks. "At least you didn't have an ill-advised one like my first romance."

Conscious of the heat rising to her cheeks, Hannah turned to straighten a harness strap that'd twisted over Daisy's flank. "Yours was no more ill-advised than mine at the time."

"I disagree. The players were completely different. Even if Atlee had married me instead of Louisa five years ago, we'd most likely be miserable by now. I think what you're most unhappy about is that you're not with the man, this Gabriel Bartel." Gail turned to lift Lily into the buggy. "Come on, sweetie. We need to get home to fix supper for *daed*." She stepped back from the rig to pin Hannah with a gaze. "Which makes me wonder why you aren't."

"*You* should know the answer to that." Hannah nodded subtly toward the little girl visible behind the windshield.

"Are you saying you broke it off with him because of me?" Gail sounded as horrified as she looked.

Hannah shrugged a defensive shoulder at the accusation. "We couldn't both leave." Seeing the instant dismay on her sister's face, Hannah reached for her hand. "I know you didn't want to go. You didn't expect the way things went with Atlee. But you didn't see what leaving did to *Mamm* and *Daed*. The reaction and whispers of some in the community. How could I leave right behind you to marry someone from outside our community? And you know as well as I do, if more than one child from a Plain family leaves to the outside, the others in the family are more likely to follow. I couldn't do that to our younger *brieder* or our folks."

Gail's smile was cynical. "The same community you just mentioned as distressing our parents by hurtful actions and gossip?"

"The same community that welcomed you back."

At the bang of a door, they turned to watch Ruby Weaver cross the porch and stride to her buggy, parked in a position of honor close to the house. "For the most part," Gail quipped.

Releasing her hand after a light squeeze, Hannah shared a smile with her sister. "You take the good with the bad."

"Well, I think you should take what would be good for you and go after your Mennonite man."

Hannah's smile instantly ebbed. "I shouldn't. I can't." She shook her head. "I'm not you."

"*Ach*, you'd have made so many more foolish mistakes if you were. It's okay to allow yourself one or two." Gail sighed. "It's just that, after so many years of being afraid and essentially alone, I'm so happy now. I just want you to be happy, as well."

"I am happy having you and Lily back in the community and with family. Maybe that's why I feel I shouldn't leave. It'd be a mistake I'm not willing to make."

"*Ja.* It's *wunderbar* to be back. Though I think it's more because of the man. It wouldn't be the same without Samuel. But I wouldn't have gone against my fears and mild—" she rolled her eyes at the understatement "—resistance at returning if I hadn't been pushed. And look what I would've missed. I was doing what I thought was best for me and Lily. But *Gott* had a plan for me. I just had to face my biggest fear."

A tapping on the windshield behind them drew their attention. They looked up to see Lily waving from inside the buggy. Wrapped in a blanket, she shivered exaggeratedly, a big grin on her face. Hannah laughed.

"I get the hint." Gail shook her head at her daughter's antics.

As she turned to go, Hannah touched her arm. "Don't worry about me. I'll be all right. Like the old saying goes, if you can't have the best of everything, make the best of everything you have. That's what I intend to do."

"*Ja*, well, don't be alarmed if *Gott* has some surprises for you along the way. And unexpected methods of bringing them about." With a wave, Gail climbed into the buggy. Hannah watched as Lily immediately scooted over and snuggled under her mother's arm.

Sniffing against an unexpected surge of melancholy as she watched the two, Hannah slowly returned the wave as Gail backed the rig out and they clattered down the lane. Upon directing Socks into her own buggy, Hannah climbed in and sat a moment, absently fiddling with the reins.

Dear Gott, *Your will is right and good. And I will trust in it.* Hannah stared through the windshield, splattered here and there with residue from its travels. Through the streaks and splotches, she considered her future. Happy in community and family, and content in her… She sighed deeply. *I will be content in my marriage.* If not to Jethro Weaver, then to some other Amish man. As she tried to envision other single men from the community, Gabe's face filled her mind, his teasing smile, his caring eyes. Hannah squeezed her eyes shut, hoping to block out his image. But what filled her head instead was a quick, unbidden plea. *Oh,* Gott, *You work in mysterious ways. If only one of those ways would lead to Gabe…*

Blinking her eyes open at the rebellious thought, Hannah backed Daisy away from the fence. It might've worked out for Gail to have the best of everything. She was thrilled for her sister.

And Hannah knew that for her, what *Gott* provided would be good, even if not necessarily everything. Besides, there was so much more to life than love. Wasn't there?

Chapter Nine

The winter sun was winking at the horizon as Gabe drove into town. These days, when the sun seemed to set in the middle of frigid afternoons as the calendar climbed away from the shortest day of the year, usually made him melancholy. But today, Gabe couldn't keep the smile from his face as he watched the purple-and-pink-streaked sky spread over the snowy landscape.

It'd been difficult, given yesterday morning's dismal news, to get enthused about today's appointments, but Gabe compelled himself to do more than just go through the motions. It wasn't his nature to be lackadaisical in his work. Besides, surely someday the town would be able to support a more robust emergency medical service. As long as he was here, he was going to lay as solid a foundation as possible for whatever might follow.

He'd been stunned when he stopped by the administration office late in the day. He'd expected to be advised on how they wanted things wrapped up. Instead, he was told another possible source of funding for the project had been proposed. By the Amish community.

When he recovered from his shock, Gabe had asked the administrator if she was kidding. The woman had primly advised him that she didn't joke. And as the Amish were usually quite successful in their fundraising—although she wasn't familiar with this particular Amish woman—the administration was willing to leave the situation open-ended for the moment to see how things played out. Further determination would be made based on how much money was raised. If Gabe had any questions, he needed to contact—the woman had checked her notes—a Hannah Lapp, who could be reached at The Stitch quilt shop in town.

After returning to the truck, Gabe had sat for a moment, staring through the windshield. He had questions all right. This was out of character for the demure Amish woman he knew. Why was Hannah doing this? His hands clenched on the steering wheel. Was it because of him? Was she trying to save his job? His heart rate picked up, as did his hopes. Was it more than just trying to extend the EMS service for the township? Could it be a sign she wanted to extend their relationship, as well?

Just the possibility filled Gabe with a warmth that surely exceeded even the glow of a sunny mid-June afternoon. It stayed with him through his last appointment of the day.

His smile expanded when, slowing for the upcoming intersection, he glanced toward the Bent 'N Dent store on the corner. Gabe touched the brakes when he recognized one of the few Amish rigs in the parking lot. The district's *Ordnung* dictated the design and color of the buggies in the community. Given they all looked the same, who'd have thought Gabe would learn to pick out Daisy from all the brown Standardbreds in the area? But seeing her numerous times behind the shop always generated a little thrill through him, as it meant her driver was nearby. He'd unconsciously memorized every minute detail of the mare and the buggy she generally pulled. The sight of Daisy at the hitching post made his pulse spike.

Daisy's owner was just the person he'd love…well, he'd love to see today.

Gabe pulled into the Bent 'N Dent's lot. When he stepped inside, he was surprised at the dimness. The store's interior, lit as it was by skylights and some lanterns, was even darker without the aid of the now-set sun. No wonder the place closed at 5:00 p.m. in the wintertime. At the checkout counter just inside the door, an older Amish woman looked him over before giving a slow nod.

"Folks come in to search for bargains. With the day drawing to an early close, you might need something to aid you in your hunt today." She handed him a flashlight, her eyes crinkling at the corners as she smiled.

Hooking a nearby basket on his elbow, Gabe took the flashlight with a matching grin. It would be a big help in scrutinizing things on the shelves. In Bent 'N Dent stores, some of the cans and cartons were just that, bent and dented. Many items were past their prime, with dates inked on the package—whether they be best by or expiration—having passed days, weeks or even months earlier. It made for a buyer-beware shopping experience. The shelves might be dark, but it was still light enough, as Gabe passed the ends of the aisles, to identify the few folks shopping this late in the day.

Besides, he wasn't looking for canned goods, he was looking for…

Gabe stopped at the end of an aisle. Hannah, her own flashlight in hand, was on the opposite end, minutely examining the can in her hand. Keeping his beam off, Gabe took a moment to just absorb the sight of her.

What was it about this woman that'd caused him to instantaneously fall for her years ago and never forget her? Certainly she was beautiful, with her golden-blond hair, deep blue eyes and exquisite features. That might've been what drew him to her in the first place. Had that weighed on him more than it should? Most men were intrigued by a pretty face. Because of his job, he'd seen enough to know that beauty was only skin deep. Besides, he'd met other beautiful women over the years and had easily forgotten them. No. That wasn't what had kept him wanting to be with Hannah again and again.

It wasn't her beauty that captivated him. At least not her outward beauty. Over the long five years without her, it wasn't her pretty face Gabe had missed, or her slender figure. It was their mutually giddy smiles. The laughs they'd shared. Her calm, quiet presence in the occasional moments when they weren't talking. Her peaceful silence, almost as precious as a solid conversation—and they'd had plenty of those. Her thoughtful perspective. Her generous encouragement. The way she filled a part of him as nothing other than saving lives did.

The Amish spoke of finding God's chosen one for them. Gabe could understand that. It would certainly be a lot easier for him if God had chosen for him someone other than Hannah, but Gabe didn't think He had.

So he'd jumped, maybe foolishly so given the current precarious job situation, at the chance to get back into her orbit so he could persuade her that they could have something together. Something wonderful. Was she finally starting to feel that, too?

Taking a deep breath, Gabe started down the aisle toward her. "Are you finding any bargains?"

Hannah's unguarded expression when she saw him told him everything he could've hoped for. They had a chance. Whatever the obstacles, they had a chance. That was all he needed to know. Enough to prevent a sigh when she quickly masked her elation with composed features and a shy smile.

"Right now, it's a bit of a challenge to find anything."

Gabe glanced in the blue plastic basket hanging from her elbow. "Looks like you found a few."

"*Ja.* Enough to make it worth the drive into town."

"I heard you've already had quite a busy one today."

Even in the darkening light through the skylights, her bewilderment was apparent.

"The fundraiser," he prompted.

Her bemusement transitioned to astonishment. "How did you find out about that so quickly?"

Gabe shook his head. "It's amazing what your community accomplishes without a phone on everyone's hip. I don't know how, but they knew in the administration office when I stopped in." He hesitated, because his next question made all the difference. "It's true? That it was your idea?"

For the span of a few heartbeats, he wondered if she'd answer. She fastidiously placed the can she held into her basket and seemed to find it fascinating before meeting his eyes again. "I'm sure if I hadn't come up with it, someone else would have. It is a *gut* thing for the community."

Raising an eyebrow, Gabe held her gaze. "Just the community?"

"Well, the *Englisch* one, as well."

"*Gut* thing." Gabe echoed her Amish dialect. "Because of it, they're delaying the ending date of the program to see how it progresses. Looks like I might not be leaving so soon after all."

Hannah's eyes rounded. "Really?" Her voice rose on the word. She immediately glanced down toward her basket again. He wasn't sure, in the dim light of the aisle, whether it was a blush or shadows that darkened her cheek.

"Really." Gabe reached out to touch her porcelain skin with a gentle finger. Hannah looked up at his touch. Gabe lost himself for a moment in what he saw there. He would have stayed frozen forever if the beam of a flashlight hadn't shot across the now-dark skylights overhead. This wasn't the place. They had observers, most likely Amish ones, an aisle over.

This wasn't the moment. But after years of wishing and wondering, Gabe now knew they'd have one. Hopefully a lifetime of them. But he still had to be patient.

Lowering his hand, he stepped back. "So, what's for supper?"

Hannah's shoulders lifted and sank in a deep sigh. "Maybe not for supper, but I did find some prizes. The breakfast bars are only a month past their 'best buy' date. My four younger *brieder* will surely have them gone in a few days. *Mamm* can hardly keep enough food around to satisfy them. I also found these cookies." She pointed to a crushed package in her basket. "They're likely smashed, but the boys won't care when they put them into a bowl and pour milk over them for dessert. What are you here to find?"

Gabe didn't say "you," but he knew his eyes did. And Hannah obviously understood, as another flush rose up her cheeks. "Actually, supper for me. I figured I'd skip The Dew Drop a few nights and give my wallet a break from eating out. Although it's pretty relieved at potentially having a few more weeks of a job. Can you help me find something to put on my limited menu?"

"What do you like?"

"Depends more on what I can find." Turning on his flashlight, Gabe directed it to scan the aisle they were in. The surrounding shelves were well-stocked. There was obviously order to the system, but Gabe couldn't identify what it was. "Unfortunately, in this, I sometimes can't see the trees for the forest. How do you find what you're looking for?"

Hannah opened her mouth, abruptly closing it when a beam of a flashlight, followed by an Amish woman, turned into the aisle. Although she kept the beam lowered, the middle-aged woman paused at the sight of them before she nodded and proceeded down the aisle, quickly evaluating and picking up a few items as she went.

Gabe braced for Hannah to step away from him in the woman's presence, to act like they weren't together. When she didn't move from his side, his shoulders relaxed and he briefly closed his eyes. Was it because Hannah was getting less concerned about what the community thought when he was with her, or was it simply because she figured it was dark enough they weren't easily recognized? Either way, it was progress.

The woman was still in the aisle when Hannah continued. "I've been navigating this and other stores like it since I was a *meedel*." Hannah moved a few steps down the aisle. "How does soup sound?" She gestured to several stacks of cans, all of them with some type of dent in their sides. "Always make sure it's dented in, not bulged out. They try to catch those, but you need to be aware."

"Got it. In, not out." Shining his light on a few nearby cans, Gabe raised his eyebrows at the prices. "Wow. These are bargains."

"*Ja*. If you're a bargain hunter, you'll have to be careful about not leaving with more than you intended."

Selecting two cans, Gabe put them in his basket. "Well, I'll just have to hope a certain someone can manage it so I can stay long enough to eat what I take."

She smiled. "Do you like spaghetti? Usually some good options on sauces here. And pasta that's not too far from the buy-by date."

"Lead on." Gabe gestured with his basket. On the other side of the aisle, he followed the beam of her flashlight when she directed it to an array of taller cans. "Oh my. You're right," Gabe murmured as he looked them over. "So what's the best bet? Big dents or little dents?"

"*Ach*, that's a serious question. It's one each person will have to make up their own mind on. I'm not sure I know you well enough to answer."

"It's okay. I trust you." After all, he was trusting her with his heart. Gabe just hoped it didn't end up the most dented of all.

A few more items, including breakfast bars for himself, went into his basket as they worked their way down the aisles. Although many cans had only a few tears on the labels, Gabe found one that had no label at all. Tipping the top toward his light, he saw, whatever the contents were, they had yet to expire.

He held the can up to Hannah. "What do you think is in here?"

She shook her head. "Hmm. I don't know. The rest of the things here are fruits. So peaches maybe? Pears?"

"My luck I'll open it, hungry for some peach halves, only to find more olives than I can eat in a year. But... then again, it could be the best thing I've ever eaten out of a can." Gabe frowned at the silver container in his hand. "What's life without some risks? We don't always know how things will turn out." He shifted his gaze to Hannah. "Sometimes you have to be brave. Sometimes things might not end like you want, but on the other hand, sometimes they might be even better. Could be missing some of the best deals if you're afraid to take a chance on the unknown." His flashlight was lowered, leaving her face in shadow. But her solemn expression revealed she understood Gabe wasn't talking about the can he tucked into his basket.

They rounded the end of that aisle and looked down the final one. "How are you set for shampoo, soap and such?"

"Pretty good. My patients haven't complained at least." He winked at her.

By tacit agreement, they headed toward the checkout. Both carried their baskets on the outside, their inside hands only a short span apart. Gabe flexed his fingers, aware that just a slight extension of them would brush Hannah's delicate ones.

"Let me know if there's anything I can do to help with the fundraiser." Gabe glanced dubiously at the items in his basket. "I wouldn't be much good at baking, but I'd be more than happy to help with other things. Community awareness, publicity among the *Englisch*, helping set up a location. You name it. Let me know." He indicated for her to go ahead of him at the cashier. "I can't thank you enough for doing this, Hannah."

She set her basket down on the counter in front of the gray-haired Amish woman manning the old-fashioned cash register. "It's *gut* for the community."

When it was his turn, Gabe pulled some bills from his wallet, glad he had cash on him as the store didn't take credit. Even seeing some of the prices, he was surprised at how low his bill was.

When he got outside, Hannah was climbing into her buggy. Gabe smiled when, inside the rig, he barely made out Socks peeking out from under a blanket.

"Gabe." Hannah paused on the buggy step and turned toward him. "It wasn't only because it was *gut* for the community." Before he could answer, the door was closed behind her. But he could see her soft smile through the windshield as she backed Daisy out.

Gabe headed for his truck, his grin big enough to light up the dreary twilight of the abbreviated winter day all by himself.

In the dim glow of her battery-powered headlamps, Hannah could see Daisy's ears flick back, alerting her that someone was behind them on the dark road. Glancing in the side-view mirrors, she saw the distant glow of headlights. Directing Daisy closer to the side of the paved country road, she waited for the whoosh of someone rushing by now they had the room. It remained silent except for the quick cadence of the mare's hooves as no vehicle passed.

For a moment, Hannah's heart leaped, thinking maybe Gabe was following her home. She craned around to look out the back. The vehicle was closer. Instead of truck lights, these were lower, nearer to the ground. It was a car. Following slowly. Her pounding heart accelerated as she shifted from excitement to trepidation. In hope of prompting the driver to pass, Hannah slowed Daisy to a walk and pulled more to the road's edge. She slid in her seat as the buggy tipped slightly toward the ditch. The car behind slowed even further.

Socks huddled next to her. Even lazy Daisy was jerking her head, impacted by the tension running down the reins. Hands clenched tightly on the leather,

Hannah guided the mare back onto the pavement and urged her to road-speed again.

When they made the final turn to their road, Hannah swung wide, hoping to get a glimpse of the vehicle. When she did, her breath hitched and she slapped the reins on Daisy's hindquarters, startling the Standardbred into a speed the mare hadn't used in some time. Hannah recognized the car that was turning onto the road behind them. It was the one that'd scraped onto the sidewalk. The one the man had sprung from. The man who'd focused his eerie attention on Socks. Had he been the one who'd taken her? Was he going to make sure she didn't get away this time?

Oh, Gabe, I wish you were here.

Dear Gott, *please protect Your servant.*

Her family's home and barn, silhouetted by the rising moon, were visible ahead. Their large, dark shapes had never looked so good.

As they charged toward that haven, Hannah began to shake, not with fear, but with anger. She was angry that someone would threaten her dog. She was angry that dogs belonging to others were lost, some only returned to their loving owners because of something called a microchip. What about the dogs that hadn't been recovered? Whose owners didn't know where they were?

Hannah gritted her teeth as Daisy pounded down the road. Someone had to do something.

Upon swinging into the lane, she pulled Daisy to a stop and set the brake. With a trembling hand, she rooted in one of the buggy's many compartments for a flashlight. Finding one, she pushed open the rig's door.

Her knees were so wobbly, she almost fell down the step. Socks jumped down behind her. Hannah urged the dog to go to the house, but the collie stayed by her side. Socks whined, but didn't bark. Dash was at the top of the lane, barking enough for both of them. Barking enough to rouse the whole neighborhood. Hannah drew strength from his indignant clamor.

She heard the bang of one of the barn doors. Hannah risked a glance in that direction to see a lantern light framed in a doorway in the area where at least some of her family would be milking. It gave her further courage.

Striding a few steps away from the buggy, she looked down the lane to see the car idling on the road at the end of it. Hannah knew it was the man from town, although she couldn't see him in the dim light. She knew, in her black cloak and bonnet, she stood out in dark relief against the snow of the lane and surrounding farmyard. Socks's warm weight snugged up against her leg.

"What do you want?" Hannah curled her fingers into the palm of her hand, wanting to force the tremor from her voice. "You're frightening me. Are you the one who took my dog? The *Biewel* says Do Not Steal. I don't know why you are doing these things, but it's not right." Something compelled her to continue, "I'm sure you don't mean to scare people. You need to stop. It's not right."

There was no response from the car. No sound except the quiet rumble of the engine. Even to Hannah's untrained ear, the sound was much smoother than the car's appearance. After a long moment, through which

Hannah could count her heartbeats from the way they throbbed in her ears, the car rolled forward. It began picking up speed as it went down the road. Seconds later, all that was visible were the red taillights in the distance.

Shaking, Hannah sank to her knees and pulled Socks to her. Her legs wouldn't hold her and she tipped to sit in the middle of the lane. Socks crawled into her lap and licked her face. An instant later, Hannah started at the nudge against the back of her bonnet. Dash joined Socks in nosing at the tears on her face. Tears Hannah hadn't been aware of shedding.

"Are you all right?" The call wafted down from the direction of the barn. Twisting on her cold seat, Hannah saw the silhouette of a figure come out of one of the doors.

Stiffly, she rose to her feet and dusted off the back of her cloak. "*Ja. Ja.* I'm *gut.*" And, oddly enough, she was. She'd faced a fear. She'd protected her dog. Something else had shifted inside of her, but she wasn't sure yet what it was.

Shuffling over, she patted Daisy's sweaty hip. She needed to get the mare to the barn. As she climbed back into the buggy, Hannah realized she'd proposed the idea of a fundraiser auction to the community and confronted a threat to her pet today.

If she could do that, what else could she face?

Chapter Ten

At the jangle from the bell above the door, Hannah looked up from where she was cutting material for project packets. Her ready smile evaporated from her face quickly when she saw who entered. Knowing she should greet the new arrival, Hannah couldn't make her feet step away from the counter. Since quilting yesterday—and her launch of the fundraising project—she'd known this encounter was possible. Make that probable. She'd been dreading it.

"Bishop Weaver." Setting down the scissors, Hannah folded her arms across her chest. It was a struggle to form her mouth into a smile. "What can I do for you today?"

The bishop slowly wove his way through the rows of fabric to reach the far side of the wide counter. Hannah furrowed her brow as he approached. Under his flat-brimmed black hat, the bishop's face was pale and dotted with sweat. Perhaps his obvious agitation was due to an ailment, but it still didn't bode well for her.

"I understand that you are getting mixed up in *En-*

glisch things, Hannah Lapp. You would do better to devote your time to convincing my son that you'd welcome an offer from him."

Hannah clenched her hands into fists. Her contrived smile slipped into more of a grimace. "I…I do." Wincing, Hannah recognized the similarity of her words to wedding vows. She would marry Jethro. Even though she cared for another man. Surely *Gott* knew she would do what she should in action, even if her spirit was reluctant?

"You should make sure he's aware of that. He says he doesn't want to marry right now."

Although relieved to not immediately discuss the auction, Hannah's heart went out to Jethro. The man was caught in the strong currents of his parents' demanding wills as much she was. Lowering her arms, she clasped her hands at her waist. "Perhaps it is a little soon," she began tentatively. "After such a recent loss of his wife and child."

"He will marry as his parents wish. As he did before. As *you* should do."

Hannah flinched as the bishop slapped his hand down, rattling the nearby scissors on the counter.

"Your duty is to do what is best for the community as I—as *Gott* wills it." Now inexplicably panting, the man leaned an elbow against the workbench when he finished his decree. At the spasm that contorted his features, Hannah circled the counter to approach him.

"Bishop Weaver, are you all right?" She gasped when the man grabbed his left shoulder. As he teetered backward, Hannah reached out a hand to guide him toward the chair kept nearby for waiting customers.

The bishop slumped hard into the seat. When he looked up at her, bewilderment and fear were evident in his face. "I don't think I'm going to make it," he whispered.

Wide-eyed, Hannah opened her mouth to assure the bishop he would be fine, only to be left gaping when he fell forward from the chair to the floor, her hand curling into his jacket to slow the tumble.

Hannah followed him down until she was on her knees beside the inert man. "Bishop Weaver! Can you hear me?" The bishop's mouth sagged open, and his eyes were rolled back in his head. He was obviously unconscious.

Unlike when Ruth collapsed, there wasn't anyone to run for assistance. Barbara had left that morning to visit her adult children living out of state. Hannah knew, as she'd been listening, that Gabe had left earlier in the day and hadn't returned. She was alone. Springing up like a jack-in-the-box, she frantically looked out the window, hoping someone was passing by on the sidewalk and could be flagged down.

The street outside the shop was empty.

The phone! Heart pounding like a runaway horse, Hannah grabbed for the landline on the counter. She fumbled with the receiver, almost dropping it as she knelt again beside the motionless man. The strident drone of the dial tone was abnormally loud in the silent room. Fingers trembling, she stabbed out 911 on the keypad.

As she waited breathlessly, the three numbers reminded her faintly of another series of three. An alphabet one. What was it? Oh yes! CPR. CAB. The C was for…? Contractions? No! What had Gabe taught her upstairs…? Compressions! That was it! And they needed to start immediately. But before that, she needed to…

Propping the handset against the base of the counter, Hannah jumped when a composed voice came over the line.

"911. Where is your emergency?"

Hannah pressed the speaker button and shifted to ease the limp bishop onto his back. "Ah, The Stitch," she responded breathlessly. "It's a shop in Miller's Creek."

"Do you have a street number?"

"Ja." Hannah searched her memory until she was able to recite it for the dispatcher.

"And what is your phone number?"

Hannah froze in her actions of unfastening the bishop's coat and tugging it back toward his shoulders. She rarely called the shop. Staring at the handset, she noticed the number taped to the inside and rattled it off.

"What is your emergency?"

"The bishop is unwell. He grabbed his shoulder and fell out of the chair."

"Is he conscious?"

"Nee, I mean no."

"Is he breathing?"

There was no discernable movement in the chest underneath her fingers. "I don't think so," she whispered.

"Stay on the line," directed the calm voice. "I'm going to get an ambulance on the way."

While the phone line was quiet—it seemed forever to Hannah but was probably only a few seconds—she tentatively started compressions. She froze after two. It was so different than working on the mannequin upstairs. Drawing in a steadying breath, she began again. After a few motions, Hannah recalled the rhythm of it. But how she missed Gabe's presence beside her and calm tutelage.

The voice came back on the line. "Does the patient have a cardiac history?"

"I don't know," Hannah responded, huffing lightly with the surprising exertion required in giving compressions. The dispatcher asked other questions that Hannah had no answer to. She wanted to weep at her ignorance, but had no time for it.

"You're doing fine," the woman advised her. "I can hear you. Do I understand you're doing compressions?"

"*Ja.* But I'm not sure I'm doing them right."

"That's okay. You're doing a great job. We'll talk you through it." As the dispatcher talked her through the process, Hannah made adjustments where needed. The woman counted with her, helping her keep her in rhythm. It wasn't long before Hannah was panting in time with the compressions. Her heavier breathing must've been audible over the phone.

"You're doing great. Help will be there very soon. Is there anyone else nearby who knows how to do CPR?"

"*Nee*, there's no one here but me." Hearing the growing whimper in her voice, Hannah cleared her throat and struggled to regain composure.

"He's fortunate you're there to help him. Any change in his condition?"

Hannah studied the slack face below hers. Were his lips slightly blue? Or had they already been that way before she started compressions and were now better? Was a little color returning to his face? Her arms were growing tired. Biting her lip, Hannah prayed for reserves of strength. Reserves she drew upon as a young woman who'd done physical labor throughout her life. *Please, Gott, help him. Please help me help him.*

Over her ragged breathing and the encouragement of the dispatcher, Hannah thought she heard the bang of the shop's alley door. Had she just imagined it? Or wished it? She had no time to wonder when Gabe burst through the door into the store. "Hannah!"

Never faltering in her rhythm, Hannah erupted into tears.

"Ma'am," the dispatcher's voice was sharp and insistent. "Are you all right?"

"Ja! Ja!" Weeping with relief, Hannah hastened to assure the dispatcher. "Help has arrived!"

Dropping to his knees, Gabe slid into place on the other side of the bishop. "This is Gabe Bartel, Miller's Creek EMS. I'm taking over CPR." Jerking a device from his key chain, he quickly used it to cover the bishop's mouth. With a motion to Hannah to pause, he gave the man two breaths.

"Copy. ETA for ambulance is 8 minutes. Dispatch is disconnecting."

"Copy."

Hannah sagged back against the base of the counter, and Gabe shifted over the bishop, taking over compressions. Hugging her weary arms, Hannah tried to ward off the trembling that instantly besieged her. She watched through tear-blurred eyes as Gabe kept up a decisive rotation of compressions and breaths.

"How long was he out before you started compressions?"

"A minute or two? It all happened so fast. It took a moment to remember what you told me. I'm sorry. It happened so fast..." Hannah knew she was babbling. In a moment, she'd be crying again, as well. She was just so glad to see him. So glad to have help. She'd been so scared.

"You did great." Gabe met her eyes. There was no mistaking the intent sincerity in their green depths. "I'm so proud of you. If he makes it, and we're going to do everything we can to make that happen, it's because of you."

Sniffing back tears in response to his encouraging smile, Hannah straightened from where she'd slumped against the counter. "What can I do to help?"

Gabe winked at her. "Atta girl. The ambulance should be here soon. Could you go outside and flag them down? Every moment helps."

"Of course." Pushing to her feet, Hannah wobbled, wincing at the tingling in her lower limbs, the result of long tense minutes in a cramped position.

Concern instantly covered Gabe's features. "You okay?"

She couldn't stop herself from reaching out to touch him as she hustled past to the door. "*Ja*. I am so much more than okay now that you're here." Jerking open the shop door, she dashed onto the sidewalk, sliding a bit on the slick, snow-swept surface. When the winter breeze ruffled the damp hair in front of her *kapp*, Hannah realized she'd been sweating. Lifting her hand to her prayer covering, she found it askew. Releasing a few deep breaths through pursed lips, the everyday task of repinning her *kapp* helped steady her.

She was just starting to feel the cold when the wind carried the beautiful sound of an approaching ambulance siren.

When she led the EMS personnel inside, it was to the welcomed sight of Bishop Weaver stirring and blinking his eyes. Ensuring she stayed out of the way, Hannah sagged bonelessly against a row of fabric, uncaring that she knocked the bolts crooked from their normally pristine arrangement.

When Gabe followed the gurney to the ambulance a short time later, she stayed inside the store, numbly watching the small crowd that'd gathered outside. A few of the onlookers were Amish, their faces mirroring shock and dismay as their bishop was loaded into the ambulance.

By the time Gabe reentered the shop, Hannah had straightened the fabric bolts, hung up the phone and shakily lowered herself into the chair by the counter. At the sound of the bell and the tread of his shoes, she surged to her feet and into his arms. She almost wept anew with relief and comfort as they closed securely about her. Her eyes fluttered closed at his light kiss on her forehead.

"You probably saved his life," he murmured into her hair.

Hannah sniffed once before succumbing to tears. They leaked onto his shirt.

Gabe rocked her gently. "Shh. It's okay. You did fantastic. His vitals were good when they left. They'll take good care of him. You did everything you could and did it well."

Hannah inhaled raggedly. "How can you do what you do? I was so frightened."

"How can I not?" Another soft kiss, this time on her hair. "If I can save one life, or help one person on what might be their worst day, I feel like I'm fulfilling a major part of the purpose God has for my life."

Her knees still shaky, Hannah snuggled closer into his embrace. She'd felt that, too. Once the fear had subsided, when the outlook had become hopeful, among the myriad of emotions that'd bombarded her had been a sliver of satisfaction in making a difference.

Gabe rocked her a moment more, before he eased back to look down into her face. Lifting a hand, he gently thumbed away the remaining tears from her cheeks. "God has a purpose for all of us. When I found mine, it was like something falling so obviously into place, I'm surprised there wasn't an audible click. I don't always save everyone." Gabe paused, his face solemn as his thoughts went somewhere far away from the brightly colored store. When he spoke again, his voice was initially hoarse. "But I do all I can to make a difference, to create a positive outcome."

He took another small step back, his arm drifting away from her shoulder. Hannah felt its absence, the loss of its warmth and support, immediately. Reaching out a hand, she grasped the back of the chair she'd been sitting on earlier. Gabe's gaze followed the movement with lowered eyebrows.

After a moment, his attention remaining on the seat, he half smiled. "I'd be careful sitting in that."

Hannah cautiously pulled her hand away, as if the chair suddenly presented a danger.

"There must be something about it. People keep passing out whenever they sit there. Of course—" his crooked smile expanded into a teasing grin "—the other common denominator is you. And that I can understand. You take my breath away whenever I'm around you."

Hannah slapped her hands to her face to cover her flaming cheeks. The action also served to hide her smile. Ducking her head, she hurried to the other side of the counter in order to get some barrier between her and Gabe. Just in case she did something foolish, like jump back into his arms.

When he gave her a wink and a wave and headed for the back door, she waved farewell. Gabe felt certain of his purpose in life. Hannah hoped she could learn to be as certain in hers. But with her hands still reveling in the feel of Gabe's gentle fingers touching her skin, it was hard to imagine that her purpose was to marry the bishop's son.

Chapter Eleven

Pausing at the back door to the quilt shop, Gabe took a deep breath. He was going to ask Hannah to join him for lunch at The Dew Drop. The question was weightier than a simple meal together. He was asking her to make a public acknowledgment of a relationship—a *possible* relationship, he reminded himself.

Although they hadn't seen each other for the past few days, she was never far from his mind. He knew Hannah felt the same as he did—that they could have something precious and rare. Gabe ran a hand through his hair. He'd also thought the same thing years earlier. And been left alone, never to see her again until earlier this month. But if she said yes to being with him today…in full view of her Amish community…

Taking another deep breath, he pushed the door open.

Hannah poked her head out of one of the many colorful aisles as he closed it behind him. Gabe's shoulders relaxed. His lips curved to share the immediate shy smile that lit her face. He couldn't stop himself from grinning. To his joy, she seemed to be content with the same. It was more than wonderful, but the action wasn't going to get him a public date.

He cleared his throat. "I was wondering how the bishop was doing." Their efforts with Bishop Weaver had been the talk of the community the past few days.

"*Gut.* He should be out of the hospital soon."

"Glad to hear it." Gabe shifted his feet and wiped his sweaty palms against the side of his pants. *Much is lost for want of asking.* "I was also wondering if you'd be interested in joining me for lunch? I'd love to hear how the auction plans are going. Besides, an endless cup of coffee at The Dew Drop would help me get through the rest of the day."

Gabe held his breath as the smile wavered on Hannah's face. His stomach dropped. She was going to say no.

Hannah's gaze darted around the shop before returning to meet his. "I could handle getting something to eat." She put a hand over her stomach. "I think."

Gabe blew out his breath in a slow, quiet stream. Knowing it would be too much, he resisted the urge to reach out and take her hand. "Are you ready?" Hannah would understand the question to mean more than if she was prepared to walk out the door.

Her slender throat worked in a swallow, but she nodded. Unable to keep the elated smile from his face, Gabe waited while Hannah put a sign on the door and donned her cape and bonnet. Then they were out on the street. Together. In public. By her choice, and not because she was worried about her missing dog.

Gabe was abnormally aware of every horse and

buggy that *clip-clopped* past them during the short walk to the restaurant. Knowing the speed of the Amish grapevine, Gabe wondered if half the community knew he was taking Hannah to lunch before they pushed open the door into The Dew Drop. If not, from the heads that swiveled in their direction when they entered, he figured they would by the time he and Hannah placed their orders. He understood enough of the Pennsylvania Dutch dialect to know they were the topic of conversation at every table they passed.

By the studied composure of her face, so did Hannah.

Hannah sighed in relief when they settled into a booth at the back of the restaurant, just outside the swinging door to the kitchen. Her face flushed as she recalled a recent lunch here with another man. She bit the inside of her cheek. There had been nothing official about her relationship with Jethro. It'd only been... strongly suggested.

The community had been receptive to the fundraiser, even though rumors were circulating that she was spearheading the event due to her interest in the man rather than the program. Surely the community could become receptive to the man? Outsiders had been accepted before—not into the church, but into the Plain community at large. Why not Gabe? He was a good man. Surely everyone could see that? And a Mennonite. There'd been a pleased rumble throughout the district about him, initiated by the Amish volunteer firefighters who'd gotten to know him.

But what kind of relationship could they have?

Knowing his passion for his work, Hannah knew Gabe wouldn't become Plain. That left…her leaving. Could she? She'd pondered it once. The answer had been a tentative yes before it became an adamant no. But with Gail now back, some of that sting was gone.

Slipping off her cloak and bonnet, Hannah tucked them into the corner of the booth's seat before turning to face the man across the table. If they could keep his job here, was there a way they could stay together in the community? She couldn't become a baptized member of the church, but if she could still see and be involved with family and friends…could she live with that?

Studying his dear face, Hannah thought perhaps she could. It felt good to be here together. In the open. Hannah's smile pushed up like daffodils in spring. It felt really good in fact.

Gabe seemed to feel the same way. His green eyes regarded her warmly. "So, how's the auction coming? Have a location? A date?" He raised an eyebrow. "Any participants?"

"*Ja*, to all three. Since it'll help the volunteer fire department, they've offered the use of the building and surrounding area for the auction. As for participants, there's been a lot of discussion. I need to confirm items so I can have posters made to hang around town."

Gabe nodded thoughtfully. "Sounds good. Sounds great, in fact. Anything I can do to help?"

"Do you know how to sew?" Hannah jested.

"Not at all. Guess you'll have to find something else for me to do."

Right now, what Hannah would like for Gabe to do

would be reach across the table and hold her hand. Was the community ready for that? Was she? Hannah flattened her hands on the wooden surface to keep from reaching for him herself.

The bang of the kitchen doors beside them made her jump. Rebecca came over, her expression as grim as Hannah had ever seen as she set water glasses on their table.

"You ready to order?"

Gabe raised his eyebrows at the normally cheerful waitress's unusual demeanor. He reached for the menus nestled behind the napkin dispenser. "Sorry, could we have another minute?" With an abrupt nod and a pasted smile, Rebecca turned toward the kitchen.

Concerned, Hannah watched as the young woman pushed through the swinging doors. Now, over the top of them, she noticed the blotchy, tear-streaked face of Rachel Mast. As she watched, Rebecca gave a comforting hug to her older sister.

Hannah frowned. "I wonder what's going on. I hope everyone is all right. You haven't been contacted about anything, have you?"

Gabe pulled his phone out and glanced at the screen. "No missed calls." Putting the phone back, he checked the device at his hip. "Doesn't look like it."

Hannah relaxed, but she was still worried. Traveling on busy roads could be risky for the slower moving buggies. Farming was a dangerous business. Accidents might be more prevalent in the busy summer season, but silos filled with grain could be treacherous. Animals could kick or injure people. The Mast girls had recently lost their *daed* to a lingering illness. It would be awful if something had happened to their *mamm* or younger *bruder*, as well.

A low rumble of male voices heralded the arrival of a group of Amish men into the restaurant. Hannah knew them all. They worked at a local business that made portable buildings. She was surprised when a few frowned at her and Gabe. While she'd expected a few raised eyebrows, their expressions leaned to unfriendliness. Visiting with the customers they passed, the group made their way to a table. Within moments, a ripple of whispers circled the room.

By the time a more-composed Rebecca took their order and delivered it, Hannah discovered she and Gabe had drawn more attention. She straightened against the back of the booth when one of the men who'd come in with the group approached them.

"Why did you tell Aaron Raber to leave for the *Englisch* world?"

Setting down his water glass, Gabe furrowed his brow, trying to recall where he'd seen the man before. "Excuse me?"

"You told Aaron Raber to go to an *Englisch* school. He's gone. He left the community."

Frowning, Gabe shook his head. "I didn't tell Aaron to go."

The man's lips flattened. Gabe couldn't recall the man's name, but he finally placed him as a volunteer fireman who'd attended one of his trainings.

"I think there must be some kind of misunderstanding," Gabe told him. The man's grave expression didn't change. "I've only seen Aaron at the department's training the other night. We spoke briefly…" *about his interest in training on gas and diesel engines, when I gave him a number to contact about it.*

His stomach churning, Gabe strangled his fork. Now he remembered the man as one who'd been in the small cluster near where he and Aaron had spoken. Surely Aaron hadn't taken Gabe's simple action as encouragement to leave?

It took another swallow to force down the previous bite of food that suddenly stuck in his throat. The goodwill of the Amish community was helpful to his job. In fact, if they were going to be the ones financially supporting it, it was vital. His gaze shifted to Hannah. It would be vital for that relationship to work, as well.

Gabe cleared his throat. "We chatted about a business interest he had. I gave him some information. That was all. I certainly didn't encourage him to leave."

The man's expression indicated he believed Gabe was directly responsible for Aaron's departure. He strode back to his companions, who were watching from their table with chilly expressions.

Gabe felt several gazes burn into his back. His meal could've been shredded paper for all he tasted. From Hannah's rounded eyes, she felt the weight of the attention, as well. When an unusually somber Rebecca passed by and gestured with the coffeepot, they shook their heads. Gabe had his wallet out before she brought over the check. Talking in the restaurant ceased as he and Hannah walked to the door. The frosty winter day outside seemed warm in contrast.

"Did you know anything about this?" Hannah whispered as they hurried down the sidewalk toward the shop.

"No more than I said at the booth. Aaron was interested in motors. Something about determining there was a need for that type of work. I gave him a contact number. Did his leaving have anything to do with Rebecca and the other young woman's distress? And why are we whispering?"

Hannah faced forward, although she spoke in a louder voice. "I've never had other Plain folks treat me like that. Not since…not for a while. It brought back memories. Unpleasant ones."

Gabe slowed his stride at her admission, but when Hannah didn't, he hurried to catch up. Before he could address her concerning comment, she spoke again.

"Everyone knows Rebecca Mast's sister Rachel and Aaron Raber are walking out together. They've been together for years. They took the baptism classes so they could be married. Aaron was supposed to be baptized with Rachel, my sister Abigail, Samuel Schrock and others this fall. Although Aaron came the day before to confirm his decision to be baptized, that Sunday morning a horse kicked him. It was obvious his arm was broken."

Gabe lifted his eyebrows. That explained the short cast on Aaron's arm the night of the training.

"They took him to Portage to have it taken care of. Benjamin came and was baptized. I don't know when they were going to complete it for Aaron. I know Rachel has been anxious, because she's waited all this time to marry him. And now he's gone."

Gabe blew out a breath. "No wonder she was upset," he murmured. "How often do young folks leave from your district?"

Hannah stumbled. Gabe automatically shot out a hand to catch her. To his surprise, she shook it off. "Not…often. Rarely. Not since…not since my sister years ago."

"Your sister left? When was this?"

"That day we were supposed to meet." Jerking open the door to the quilt shop, Hannah swept inside, leaving Gabe rooted to the sidewalk.

By the time he followed, she'd hung up her cloak and positioned herself behind the counter, almost as if she wanted a barrier between them. *Why not?* Gabe stopped on the other side. There always had been. Maybe, even beside the differences in religious doctrines, they were getting to the root of it. It certainly wasn't about their compatibility and the way he felt about her. And the way he thought she'd felt about him.

"Was that why you didn't show up that night?"

Hannah picked at the embedded ruler in the countertop. "I walked with her down the lane, trying to convince her to stay. She was determined to go. The man she'd been—" Hannah shot a glance at him from beneath lowered lashes "—secretly walking out with was marrying another, and Gail was going to have a *boppeli*."

Her voice had dropped so much that Gabe leaned over the counter to hear the last bit.

"I…I had to tell *Mamm* and *Daed*. I had never seen them so heartbroken." Hannah shifted from fiddling with the ruler to spinning the orange-handled scissors that lay nearby with her finger. "I couldn't leave them that night. Not when I was secretly meeting someone, as well."

"Why didn't you let me know?"

"How? We didn't exactly plan beyond a meeting at a time," she countered softly. "Besides, after seeing what Gail's leaving did to my family… Their sadness, the shame they felt when those who are prone to judge in the community slighted or gossiped about us. How could I do the same thing to them? How could I have left, as well? Break their hearts again? Provide more fodder for the gossips? What example would that set for my *brieder*?" Her voice grew stronger as she spoke. Hannah looked up now, eyes glistening with tears but the set of her jaw almost daring Gabe to refute her statements.

"Theirs weren't the only hearts involved," he murmured.

Hannah sniffed, her face softening. "I thought you could handle it."

Gabe's lips twitched. "I appreciate your confidence in me. I guess." Twisting to look behind him, he located the chair. "Glad you didn't remove it. I feel like I need it. I'll try not to pitch onto the floor." Stepping back, he dropped into the seat.

Hannah smiled faintly, her eyes telling him she appreciated his attempt at humor. Glad someone did. Gabe heaved a sigh, recalling his own heartache when she never showed, when his attempts to find her failed, when, despondent, he went home, and his little brother died soon after.

"So where does that leave us?" Needing something

to do when he wanted to jump up and plead his case, Gabe reached down to wipe moisture, residue of some snow on the sidewalk, from his shoes. Ears tuned to her, he could hear Hannah quietly breathing. *Say something. I love you. But I can't make this relationship work on my own.* He closed his eyes. *And I don't know if I can handle having my heart broken again.*

He snorted ruefully. Maybe there *was* something about this chair's effect on people. Opening his eyes, Gabe pushed up from it to find Hannah standing silently on the other side of the counter. Eyes wet with tears, her hands were pressed to her mouth.

"Your sister's back now, isn't she? So am I. For the moment. Do you think maybe there's a reason that God has given us this second chance?" Shaking his head, Gabe started for the back door, the silence ringing behind him.

Chapter Twelve

Hannah stopped the sewing machine's wheel and her feet paused on the treadle at the angry rattle against the windows. She glanced out at the snow gusting down the street. All afternoon the wind had been battering the windows as if it was trying to blow through the glass.

Frowning, she clipped off her thread. Her *daed* had warned her about the weather. Even cautioned that maybe she shouldn't go to work today. But since Barb had left the store in her care while she was out of town, Hannah didn't want to close it in her employer's absence.

She was thankful she'd left Daisy back at the farm. The trip home over unplowed country roads would've worn the old mare out. The topic of conversation of the few customers she'd had since noon had been the deteriorating weather and the concern they hadn't seen the worst of it yet. Hannah frowned at the snow, blowing so hard the bank's sign across the street was barely visible. A glance at the wall clock revealed it to be an hour to closing. Even Barb would agree it was reasonable to shut the shop for the day.

The window rattled again. As she pushed her chair back from the sewing machine, Hannah bit her lower lip. She needed to call the Thompsons and arrange for a ride home. Hopefully the *Englisch* drivers were willing to go out in these conditions.

She glanced up at the ceiling. She'd heard Gabe come in a short while ago. They hadn't spoken in the past two days she'd been at work, although she'd thought about what he'd said...and that she hadn't responded. Even though he'd frequently stated that much was lost for want of asking, given the current circumstances, asking him for anything was something Hannah couldn't do.

She stared unseeing at the fabric lined up under the sewing machine's presser foot. Due to some rumblings in the community about an *Englischer*'s—Gabe's—alleged involvement in Aaron Raber's absence, the auction was at a standstill. The naysayers had been quick to speak out, which had suppressed the support of others. It was no surprise who the naysayers' leader was. Even though Gabe's work had saved Bishop Weaver's life, the man's wife surreptitiously campaigned to quash the fundraising event.

Hannah didn't know how or whether to proceed. What if it was *Gott*'s will that it be ended?

No auction meant no job for Gabe.

His leaving would remove temptation, so she could focus on what she should be doing. Who she should be intending to marry. Still, the knowledge that in less than two weeks she might never see him again gnawed at Hannah's stomach and made her eyes sting.

There was a brief lull in the wind. Hannah lifted her head at the creak of the building's stairs. A moment later, the back door opened and Gabe poked his head into the shop.

"I didn't see Daisy out back." At another big gust, he looked beyond Hannah to the window. "It's getting pretty rough out there. How are you getting home?"

Hannah couldn't prevent the catch in her breath at the sight of him. She barely managed to keep her face composed. "Ah, I was going to call the Thompsons to hire them for a ride."

"Their car might have a rough time in these conditions. I'll give you a ride home."

Stepping the rest of the way into the shop, Gabe kept his attention on the windblown street. Was he intentionally avoiding her? He had reason to, after the way they'd last parted. Although she nodded solemnly, Hannah's pulse accelerated.

"It's supposed to get worse." Gabe finally looked in Hannah's direction. "How long do you need to stay?"

Hannah sprang up from her chair. "I can be ready to go in a few minutes."

"I'll go grab my gear, then head out to warm up the truck. Meet you in back?"

"Ja." Hannah dashed for the front of the store to grab her cloak and bonnet from their peg and lock the door. Quickly addressing other tasks to close the store for the night, she locked up the shop's back door and headed out.

The alley door was like a live thing, trying to jerk

out of her hands. Once outside, Hannah gasped to re-
claim some air before the wind whisked it all away.
She hopped down the path Gabe had made through
the knee-deep snow to reach the truck's passenger
door and climb in.

Directing some heat vents toward her with one
hand, Gabe hooked a thumb toward the back seat with
the other. "There's a blanket and an extra coat in back."
He returned his hands to the steering wheel and, moments later, they were heading out of the alley. The
wipers barely kept pace with the constant bombard-
ment of white.

Hannah twisted to retrieve the lap-size blanket from
the back seat. It could be that Gabe's curtness was due
to the dangerous conditions of the trip. Maybe it was
just her remorse, but his demeanor seemed almost as
chilly as the weather.

"It's worse in the country," he murmured as he
leaned forward to peer through the windshield. "I'm
glad you didn't drive Daisy today. This weather is
nothing to mess around with. How'd you get in?"

"I caught a ride in with a neighbor." Hannah was
just relieved they were talking. She didn't care what
the subject was.

By the time she'd tucked the blanket around her
legs, they'd reached the edge of town. Once the protection of the buildings was gone, the truck shuddered
under the onslaught of the buffeting winds.

Hands never leaving the wheel, Gabe darted another glance at her. "Buckle up."

Doing as he directed, Hannah kept her eyes on the
white world beyond the windshield. She didn't know

how Gabe even knew where the road was, but somehow he kept on it. They crept down the highway leading out of town at a speed her mare Daisy could've outpaced. Even so, Hannah gasped softly every time she felt the truck shift abruptly on the road's treacherous surface. Numerous times she glanced over to Gabe, taking comfort in his focused profile and capable hands on the wheel.

They both jumped when Gabe's pager went off. Finding his way into the nearest driveway, Gabe put the truck in Park and contacted the dispatcher. Following their succinct conversation, he turned to Hannah with a frown.

"I have to respond to a call. I don't have time to take you home beforehand."

"That's…that's all right. You do what you need to do."

With a terse nod, Gabe carefully backed onto the road. Hannah caught her breath and braced a hand against the dashboard when Gabe gently braked and the truck continued to slide backward. She waited until he had their forward motion under control before speaking.

"Accident?"

"Yeah. Fortunately just a little farther up the road." They crept along until Hannah could make out dark shapes against the otherwise uninterrupted white world outside, one car tipped in the ditch on both sides of the road. Putting on his hazard lights in addition to the flashing blue on the dash, Gabe parked at a 45 degree angle on the road to try to block the scene.

Leaving the engine running, Gabe's eyes were riveted on the cars as he grabbed his jump bag. "I might need your help." He glanced at Hannah, his green eyes grave. "For now, stay put."

Easing the driver's door open, he and the wind battled for control of it. Gabe won, but in the short skirmish, frigid air swirled through the cab. Hannah gasped at its vicious bite. She watched anxiously through the window as Gabe fought his way to the car on his side of the road.

When he stepped away from the road's shoulder, he sank to his knees in the snow. With a few lunging strides, he reached the driver's door of the partially buried vehicle. Clearing the snow away, he wedged it open and leaned in.

Fixated on the vehicle, Hannah's eyes widened. Even under these conditions, she recognized the older model car that'd been idling at the end of her lane that night. Heart clenching, she automatically looked around for Socks before remembering she'd left the collie at home today. Hands clasped to her chest, she stared at where Gabe was barely visible in the open driver's door. She caught her breath when he reappeared out of its depths and motioned for her before disappearing again.

Hannah hesitated as she recalled her fear as the car in the ditch had idled at the end of her lane, her anguish when Socks was missing, presumably taken by this man. A moment later, grimacing with trepidation, she pushed open the truck's door. Driving snow stung her face, and the wind whipped her cloak as she worked her way to the ditch. The tracks where Gabe had made his way down were already drifting over.

Taking a step, Hannah gasped as wet and cold gripped the thick stockings on her leg.

Gabe ducked back out of the car when she reached him. He scanned her face. "You doing okay?" he shouted above the wind. Hannah didn't know if she was nodding or shaking, but Gabe took it as an affirmative. "I'm so sorry to get you into this, but I need to get his bleeding stopped and check the occupants of the other car. Can you keep pressure on this?"

Ducking with him out of the wind, into the cavity of the car's interior, Hannah saw a man—the man who she'd seen on the street—slumped in the front seat. He was bleeding from the face and head. With a gloved hand, Gabe had a wad of gauze pressed against the man's forehead. Using his free hand, Gabe pulled another medical glove from his pocket and handed it to her.

"Here, put this on. Then I need you to take my place. Ready?" In the cramped situation, they managed to switch positions. "Head wounds bleed a lot. It's not as bad as it looks, but we still have to get it stopped. I'll check the other car and be back as soon as I can. Local police should be here soon and maybe can relieve you." He met her eyes. "You going to be okay with this?"

"Ja." Hannah nodded. As the cold seeped into her feet through her sensible black shoes, she reminded herself that she'd saved a life with Gabe's help a few days ago. She could do this, too.

"You're amazing." Touching her shoulder, Gabe gave her a smile before ducking out of the car's interior.

Even in the frigid surrounding, his parting actions warmed her. Her heart rate steadied with the knowledge of his confidence and support. Turning her focus to the man in front of her, Hannah's brows furrowed as she scrutinized his face. Under the rivulets of blood that tracked down it, the man's skin, instead of being pale with cold, was flushed. Tentatively, she held the backs of her ungloved fingers to an unbloodied space on the man's opposite cheek. Heat radiated into her cold hand. The man was burning up.

When his eyes suddenly fluttered open, Hannah jerked her hand back from his cheek. Only an arm's length apart, she could see some lucidity drifted into their depths.

One corner of the man's lips twitched slightly. "I'm sorry," he murmured. "About your dog."

With the wind buffeting the outside of the car, Hannah wasn't sure she heard correctly. Or if he was even fully coherent. "Hang on. Help is here. We'll get you taken care of."

"I didn't mean to scare you. I…" He sucked in a shuddering breath. "I took care of the dogs when I took them. I tried to find good homes for them. I just needed money to pay for the painkillers…the drugs. Drugs that have…wrecked my life. I'm sorry. So, so sorry." His eyes drifted closed again.

Memories of the sleepless night, the panic and angst of Socks's disappearance flooded Hannah. She never wanted to relive that night. And Socks had only returned because she'd chewed through a rope to escape. Hannah could've lost her forever. "Hello? You probably need to stay awake. Hello?"

The man's eyelids slowly lifted again. He regarded her with dull eyes.

Hannah forgot the wind and the cold as she looked into them. They were filled with obvious pain. Pain that wasn't just physical.

Squeezing her eyes shut, Hannah swallowed as she reflected upon the fear and anguish this man had caused her. She wasn't sure what else she could do for his physical aches, but she knew what she had to do for the other. For both of them.

Opening her eyes to meet his listless ones, Hannah whispered, "I forgive you."

The man's eyes widened. The corners of his mouth lifted slightly, and his shoulders sagged further against the seat as his eyes drifted shut again. While still flushed, he looked…peaceful. Surprisingly, it was a peace she shared.

Hannah's hand was cramped with cold. Glancing through the windshield, she was surprised to see flashing red-and-blue lights against the snow. Her relief knew no bounds when she could make out Gabe, bent almost double against the wind, cross the road toward her. She gasped when he slipped at the edge of the ditch, sliding down its length before regaining his feet. One side of him was caked in white when he ducked beside her to lean into the car.

"How're we doing?" With a glance at Hannah, he took over applying pressure. Gently lifting the gauze, he checked the wound. "The good news is the bleeding stopped." He ran his eyes over the man, lingering on a grubby bandage on the man's ungloved hand.

"Mr. Weathers, did you ever see your doctor about your dog bite?"

The man's head weakly wobbled back and forth on the headrest.

"Looks like it's gotten infected. You've got a fever and, I imagine, feel pretty lousy. There's an ambulance en route. I can't make you go to the hospital, but you're very sick, Mr. Weathers."

The man's cracked lips barely moved in his whisper. "I'll go. I was heading for the doctor, but got stuck in the lane. When I gunned it to get out, I shot onto the road and hit something. Are they all right?"

"Yes, sir, they're going to be fine. Getting a ride back into town with the officer."

Hannah could hear the faint sound of a siren. So apparently could the man. His eyes popped open and fixed on her.

"Take care of the puppies."

Chapter Thirteen

Hannah's brow creased. Was he talking about Socks? About dogs he'd taken, in general? Was he simply delirious with fever? Frowning, she caught Gabe's eye. He shook his head, apparently not understanding what the man meant, either.

"There's two. A friend of mine had them. Their momma died and he couldn't handle them. They're in the kitchen. I've been taking care of them. But…" The man was quiet for a moment as Gabe addressed the wound on his head. "I'm going to be away for a while. I…I need help. It's…it's time I got help."

Impulsively, Hannah grasped the man's grubby hand, startled again at the heat of it against her cold fingers. "Don't worry. I'll take care of the puppies. You just get better." She felt the subtle pressure as the man gently squeezed back.

"Thank you," he sighed, his hand dropping open as if the action was too much for him.

Through the windshield, Hannah caught sight of movement as people in reflective gear descended the ditch. Ducking out of the car's interior to give them room, she stumbled a few feet away through the drifts, blinking against the sting of the snow on her face. She thought she heard Gabe yell something about the truck before the wind whipped his words away. Grasping handfuls of dead grass that barely topped the snow, she pulled herself out of the ditch. Gabe's truck was now among a trio of light-pulsing vehicles. Hannah was glad to see an ambulance was one of them.

Slipping across the slick pavement, she reached the truck and battled the passenger door open to climb inside. She almost wept with relief at the warmth of the cab and break from the incessant wind. When Gabe opened the driver's door to a flurry of flakes and a blast of cold air a few minutes later, Hannah still had her fingers tucked against the blasting heat vent.

"You doing okay?" Gabe stashed his ever-present black bag behind the seat before giving her a quick survey.

Hannah nodded toward where her legs were tucked under the dash. "I can finally feel my feet again."

Gabe frowned. "I'm sorry about that. You aren't dressed for this. I shouldn't have called you out to help."

"*Nee.* I'm glad you did. I—" she ducked her head "—I'm glad you trust me to do so. I'm sorry about the other day…"

Stripping off a glove, Gabe reached for her hand. "Hannah, I don't give up easily."

Lifting his hand, Hannah touched the back of it against her cheek. Though not extremely warm, it was a compelling contact against her chilly skin. Gabe's presence in her life was like that. It added a warmth, a vibrancy, that didn't otherwise exist for her. "I'm glad about that, too."

She returned their clasped hands to her lap. "I need to get the puppies."

"Yes, ma'am." Gabe grinned at her before turning his attention to the two other vehicles maneuvering to turn around on the highway. Their flashing lights dimmed in the growing dusk and blowing snow as they pulled away. His smile faded. "The deputy said to get back into town as soon as possible. They're stretched thin and having trouble getting around themselves." He looked at Hannah, his expression solemn. "They're closing down the highway. I don't know that I'll be able to get you home, especially if the country roads are worse than this."

Hannah hissed in a breath at the dilemma. Staying with Gabe was out of the question. As a single woman, she couldn't stay overnight alone with a single man. And a single man who wasn't Amish? Her folks would be upset. Even the more open-minded ones in the community would be appalled. As for Jethro and the bishop… Well, it wasn't possible.

"The Thompsons said I could stay with them if I ever needed." Hannah liked the *Englisch* couple who frequently drove for the Amish. "But I don't know about taking puppies there."

"You fill me in on what to do. I'll take care of them at my apartment until you can get back to town. I need to call into dispatch and tell them I'm finished here." With a squeeze of her hand, he freed his to reach for the radio clipped to the driver-side visor. After Gabe advised the situation was wrapped up and they were heading back to town, he reattached it.

"I wish I could let my folks know I was all right. They would've expected me by now."

"Do you have the number of their closest phone hut? We can give them a quick call before we head in." Gabe reached for a side pocket of his pants.

Hannah's gaze sharpened when Gabe shifted abruptly to use both hands in an apparent search. Her heart rate accelerated at his grim expression as he quickly checked other pockets.

"My phone." Gabe's voice was flat as he plucked at an open flap along the edge of his pants. He closed his eyes in obvious frustration. "I'm going to check the car. If I'm lucky, I'll find it in there." Opening his eyes, he puffed out his cheeks. "If I'm not, it probably slipped out when I slid down the ditch." They both looked out the window to where the wind had already filled in the furrow created by his slide down the incline. "And someone will find it in the spring."

With a glance at her face, Gabe hooked a rueful smile. "I won't be long." Once more, wind blasted through the cab when the door opened. Tucking the blanket she'd retrieved more closely about her legs, she watched as a small light bounced around the interior of the stranded car. When Gabe emerged a short time later, she tensed, only to sag against the seat when he waved his arms in obvious failure in his search.

After a brief battle with the wind over the door, Gabe lunged into the truck. He brushed the snow out of his hair. "It's not there. I'm sorry."

Aware of his obvious distress, Hannah reached out

to touch his arm. "Why are you apologizing to me? Having a phone is more of a shock to my life than not having one." Her heart hiccupped when he shared her smile. "When I get to the Thompsons, I'll leave a message for my folks that I'm all right. That way, they'll know when someone goes to check."

"Sounds like a plan." Gabe carefully backed the truck on the highway until his headlights picked up a snow-filled lane. Two perpendicular lines along its length had been blurred to insignificance by the relentless wind. Reaching over to shift something in the console, he sighed deeply. "I hope four-wheel drive can get us out. Otherwise we'll be spending the night here, and I can't guarantee the accommodations. Hang on. It's going to be a bit of a ride."

He wasn't joking. Hannah gripped the handhold next to the ceiling as the truck bucked its way up the lane. They finally made it to the top, where even the driving snow couldn't make the house and nearby building look less dilapidated.

Upon shifting into Park, Gabe kept the engine running. "I'll get them."

Hannah already had her hand on the door handle. "I'm going with you."

She followed in his footsteps along the unshoveled walk. On the porch, they stomped their feet against the worst of the snow and entered the front door. Although not cold, it was definitely cool in the house. Having been there before, Gabe led the way to the dimly lit kitchen. In a large box tucked in the corner of the room, two black-and-white puppies snoozed and cuddled together on an old blanket.

Hannah knelt next to the box. "Oh, you sweeties!"

"Looks like Border collies. How old do you think they are?"

One of the pups lifted its head and yawned. "About four weeks, I'd say." Reaching out a hand, Hannah stroked a finger down the white strip between its little ears.

Gabe was nosing around the shabby kitchen. "I see some supplies here. What do we need to take with us to get them through the night and maybe the next day? I've got blankets, and probably a box, at the apartment."

Hannah was relieved to see that, unlike the kitchen, the pups seemed to be in good shape. Reluctantly, she rose and looked toward where Gabe stood by a counter crowded with many things, among them, fortunately, puppy supplies. "Definitely some of the milk supplement." She spied an open bag of puppy food. "Looks like he's started them on solid food. We'll need that, too. We'll mix it with the supplement. Um…do you have some type of flat pan or bowl they can eat from at your place, or do we need to bring this one?" She toed the empty bowl on the floor by the box.

"I think I'm good. Don't want to take more than we can carry." Gabe met Hannah's gaze across the dimly lit room. "Just in case," he added grimly.

Nodding at the implicit direction to hurry, Hannah turned back to the pups. "If you can grab the supplies, I've got the pups." Kneeling again, she scooted her hand under each warm little body. Mr. Weathers might not have taken care of himself, but he'd taken care of his young charges. Squirming, the pups squeaked at being rousted from their home. She clutched them to her chest as Gabe secured her cloak to ensure they were covered. When he paused, Hannah glanced up to meet his smiling green gaze. The look in them was as warm as the precious bundles she held. When she smiled hesitantly, Gabe leaned in and gave her a quick kiss on the lips.

Before she could do more than blink, he'd turned to gather the requested supplies from the counter. "Ready?"

He meant to go out the door with him and face the snow storm. Momentarily rooted on the dingy linoleum, Hannah realized she was ready for a lot of things. Including facing whatever storms might come in order to have a life with the man who currently shared a stranger's shoddy kitchen with her.

"Ja," she whispered, exhaling a breath she hadn't been aware of holding.

Supplies gripped in one hand, the other under Hannah's elbow to support her, Gabe led them to the still-running truck. The pups, awakened from the trip over the yard, yipped softly and began nosing their way out of the opening of her cloak as she settled into the seat. Although her lap was warm with the pups there, Hannah frowned when she extended a snow-dusted foot under the dash. The fan was blowing, but the truck's heater was making little headway against the biting cold outside.

Gabe shifted it into gear. "Hang on. Although we have better tracks to follow, the trip out might not be much better than the one in."

They jolted down the lane, windshield wipers battling furiously against the driving snow, then lurched from the end of the lane onto the highway. Hannah's sigh of relief morphed into gasps when the truck kept skidding over the slippery surface.

Gabe wrestled it into control. A moment later, they were creeping back toward town. If Hannah thought the trip out had been slow and treacherous, the return in the gathering darkness was more so. When a collection of weakly glowing lights, as opposed to sporadic ones indicating an *Englisch* farmyard, was visible through the blowing snow, she knew they were approaching Miller's Creek.

Trying to relax tensed muscles, she looked over in question when Gabe made a slow, careful turn into a lane, this one shorter and fortunately plowed sometime during that day.

"The Thompsons. But it's not looking good that they're home."

Gabe's concern was warranted. Hannah stayed in the truck when he went to the door and watched as he knocked once, twice, thrice. No answering light came on throughout the house's dark interior.

Gabe sighed when he got back into the truck. "I doubt they'd mind you staying, but unlike Amish homes, they keep theirs locked. Now what?"

Hannah stroked a hand over the again slumbering puppies. "I don't know when these two have last eaten. We need to get them someplace warm and feed them. I can stay in the shop." She smiled wryly. "I have access to plenty of blankets. That way I can help you with the puppies. They need to eat every six hours or so."

"If you're sure?"

"*Ja*, I'm sure."

They crept out onto the road again. "Almost there." Gabe glanced over to give her a reassuring smile.

As he negotiated a sweeping curve in the road at the edge of town, a brutal gust of wind hit them, pushing the truck sideways. Immediately, Gabe responded to correct the slide, but the icy surface had them in its grasp. His efforts to counter their careen toward the ditch were futile. Hissing in a breath, Hannah clutched the seat belt that secured her with one hand as she curved her body over the puppies to protect them. She stiffened her legs, as if the action could somehow stop the truck's spin. Wide-eyed, she watched as they skidded toward the ditch and its sharp decline.

Chapter Fourteen

The truck shuddered beneath Hannah as it left the road, skittering over the shoulder and into the ditch. The pickup rocked hard to a halt, ending at a slant toward the passenger's side. Items on the center console tumbled into Hannah as she hovered over the puppies. Something black flew across her vision to crash into the window. She'd slid over the seat, her grip on the seat belt saving her from being plastered against the door. Out her window, the only thing Hannah could see beyond it was the wind-curled top of a snowbank.

"Are you all okay?" Even competing with the moan of the wind and the rumble of the engine, the urgency in Gabe's voice was unmistakable.

Heart rocketing, Hannah took stock of her little passengers. Running a gentle hand over them, she could feel little paws press into her lap as they stretched. One climbed up her cloak to sniff at the ribbon of her *kapp* that dangled on the outside of her cloak.

"*Ja.* I think so." She tried to lean away from the

door, only to find that gravity kept a possessive hold on her. "But I seem to be stuck."

"It's okay. We'll figure this out."

Hannah twisted in her seat to unbuckle the belt now restricting her movements. With feet pressed in the foot wheel and one hand on the steering wheel to brace him, Gabe reached across the console with his other to help. They both froze when the truck creaked and shifted toward the downslope of the steep ditch.

Hannah couldn't seem to find any air. "Is it…going to tip?" she whispered.

With a grunt, Gabe maneuvered in his seat until he was leaning his weight against the driver's door. Mouth flattened into a thin line, he scanned the snow-enshrouded dusk outside the windshield. Hannah gasped as a blast of wind shook the vehicle. As the truck creaked again, Hannah slid a fraction of an inch closer toward her door. With a shared wide-eyed gaze, they both held their breaths.

Gabe's heart squeezed at the fear he saw in Hannah's eyes. He had gotten her into this. If anything happened to her because of him…

He wasn't going to try to drive out. Any rocking motion to get traction in the snow could tip them over. Their tailpipe could be covered already. If it wasn't cleared, the cab could fill with carbon monoxide. If he couldn't keep it cleared, they'd need to shut off the truck. The pickup was shelter from the wind, but not from the cold without the heater. Even with the engine running and the fan full blast, frigid air was seeping in from every corner.

Conventional wisdom was to stay with the vehicle. Biting the inside of his cheek, Gabe narrowed his eyes at the lights that heralded the homes and businesses of town. Downtown and his apartment lay just beyond. A short distance, but was he foolish to even consider trying for it? Would he be risking their lives if they left the shelter of the vehicle?

The truck shuddered under another gust. Hannah's face paled beneath her black bonnet.

Glancing at the gauges, Gabe shut off the truck and withdrew the keys. Without the comforting rumble of the engine, the wail of the wind was unobscured.

"I don't like our options. We have shelter here, but not enough fuel to last the night. If the truck tips…" Gabe pressed his lips together. He wished he was certain he wasn't making a mistake with their lives. He nodded toward the windshield. "Can you see the lights of town?"

Hannah nodded hesitantly.

Gabe rubbed his forehead. "I normally wouldn't recommend this… We can't call out with my phone gone and, if I'm not mistaken, the radio in pieces at your feet. Hard telling how long we'd be here before help can arrive. I haven't seen another vehicle on the trip back into town. If they've closed the roads, we probably wouldn't.

"But if the truck tips, we might then be dealing with injuries." He nodded toward the puppies that were investigating Hannah's lap. "They have needs we can't meet here." Gabe regarded her grimly. "I can walk in and try to find help…"

Hannah drew in a breath as her gaze darted about

the cab. "I'd rather not stay here alone. I think… I'd prefer level ground. With you." She gave him a tremulous smile, although Gabe could see it was with effort. "Even when a bad storm would blow up, the cows still need to be milked. We always made it to the barn to take care of the livestock. Of course—" the bow under her chin bobbed as she swallowed "—the barn wasn't quite so far from the house."

"I'll get you to safety." Or he'd die trying, Gabe vowed.

It was agreed. They cautiously maneuvered to gather what they'd need and could carry. Using empty grocery bags Gabe had left in the truck, they condensed the puppy supplies to what they figured would be immediately necessary. Hannah carefully wiggled into Gabe's spare coat, the sleeves long enough to cover her hands to protect them from the cold. A bungee cord used by Gabe while moving his possessions to the apartment was discovered in the console.

Every time the truck rocked under a strong gust, he and Hannah stared at each other with bated breath.

"The wind should be at our backs, which will help. Once we get among buildings, they'll block some of its force." Gabe gazed out the window toward the lights of town. "We're close enough we won't lose direction." He looked back to Hannah. "And you won't lose me. But it will be dangerously cold." Gabe's stomach clenched. He'd seen situations where people had died of exposure within yards of help. Even wearing the extra coat, he eyed Hannah's thick stockings and bonnet doubtfully, and he asked, "Will you be okay in those?"

She nodded with a half smile. "Try riding in an un-heated buggy for a couple of hours. I'll be fine."

Across the confines of the tilted cab, Gabe regarded her. Nose red with cold, hair strands straggling from under her bonnet, eyes cautious but calm, delicate hands peeping from outsize sleeves holding two wig-gling puppies clutched to her chest. She'd never looked more beautiful.

"You know, I thought you were wonderful when I met you. I've now realized I had no idea how *wunder-bar* you really are."

Hannah ducked her head, pressing her cheek against one of the pups. "I…I feel the same."

A blast of wind battered the truck again. Gabe shot a hand to the dash as he felt the vehicle lift off its driver's-side wheels. Hannah squeaked, her mouth open in an unvoiced cry. When the truck bounced back down again, Gabe blew out a breath. Slipping the strap of his jump bag to sling over his chest, he adjusted it so he could unzip his coat and fleece vest. Upon tucking his vest into his belt, he reached a hand toward Hannah.

"Let's go. Give me the babies."

She handed up the puppies one at a time. Gabe carefully tucked them into his vest, resting miniature paws against his chest on both sides before he zipped it up. He then zipped up his coat, ensuring there was room at the neck for air to reach his young passengers.

"Ready?" He winced as she pushed the blanket aside. "I wish we could take that along, but I think it'd blow around and be more in the way. Okay, I'm going to open the door and ease out. When I'm out, I'll dangle the bungee cord across the seat, and you can use it to lever out, as well." He gave Hannah what he hoped was a reassuring smile and not the grimace of concern he was feeling.

Heart pounding so hard he figured the pups pressed against his chest felt it, Gabe grasped the door handle and clicked it open. Bracing his feet in the driver's footwell, he wedged it open. The wind howled, pushing back. With a grunt, Gabe swung his legs out of the truck, shifting until he found secure footing. The wind slammed the door against him. Gabe winced at the bite of his shins against the truck. Pressing his backside firmly against the quaking door, he reached back into the cab for Hannah.

Down the slant of the truck, Hannah's face revealed the trust that struggled to overcome her fear. Gabe's heart stumbled. When they were out of this, he was going to do everything he could to ensure he was never involved in distressing her again.

Shaking the cord toward Hannah, he raised his voice so she could hear him over the howling wind. "Always knew life with you would be an adventure."

At his words, some of her fear dissipated as she wrapped one hand around the cord and used the other to lever herself along the dash. The bags of supplies were hooked on her elbow. "I could do with a little less adventure right about now."

Braced by Gabe, Hannah climbed up the seat and over the console and was soon situated beside Gabe in the wedge of the driver's door. At their first step away from the shelter of the truck, they were almost knocked to their knees by the gusts at their back. With one of Gabe's arms supporting his passengers, the other hand gripping Hannah's elbow, they climbed out of the ditch. Finding some traction on the road's shoulder, they stumbled ahead of the wind.

The snow drilled into the back of Gabe's head. Air rushed past so fast that it was hard to get a breath, and when he did gasp one in, the cold bit all the way down his windpipe. After what seemed hours but was probably merely minutes, the wind, though still fierce, was hampered by the intermittent buildings. As they got farther into town, its power decreased. Soon they were walking upright. And faster. The road surface, while covered with snow, wasn't as slick underneath.

Under his gloved fingers, Gabe could feel Hannah shivering. He had to get her to shelter. Heat. Dry clothes. All of which he had in his apartment. Gabe's hand tightened at the thought of wrapping his fingers around a hot cup of coffee. He wanted to cheer when they reached their block of Main Street.

"Just about there," he encouraged Hannah, thrilled that he could speak at a normal decibel instead of shouting against the wind.

Before heading for the alley entrance, they stopped a breathless moment to look down Main Street. It was the first time Gabe had seen it empty of cars. Even in front of The Dew Drop, the parking spaces were deserted. Soft lights glowed from inside the windows, although the restaurant looked empty. The streetlamps shone down on the deepening snow, falling flakes looking like crystals as they drifted into their feeble light.

The fabric shop was illuminated from inside, as well.

"Oh dear, I forgot to turn them off when I left."

Gabe moved his hand from her elbow to wrap it around her shoulders. "That's okay. It looks pretty good to me. It's welcoming us home."

"First thing I want to do is call the phone hut near my folks and let them know I'm okay."

"Sounds like a plan. After you use it, I hope Barb won't mind that I borrow it to check in."

"I'm sure that would be fine…" Hannah's words died off as everything suddenly went dark about them. The street lights, the shop's lights, the lights from The Dew Drop. The street was pitched into darkness, the only light the white of the snow.

Chapter Fifteen

"What happened?" Hannah's voice was shaking as much as her slender shoulders were under his arm.

"Power went out." Gabe tucked her closer to his body.

"Will it come back on? It's not a factor at home, but so many things here depend upon it."

"It will, but I don't know when. Come on, let's get you inside." Gabe urged Hannah around the corner to the alley entrance. Supporting the squirming pups inside his jacket with one arm, Gabe kicked snow away from the door in order to get it open enough for them to stumble through. The hall inside was pitch black and silent. A silence broken by Hannah's surprising giggle.

"I'm just so happy to be here."

"Probably not as happy as I am to have gotten you here. Still, we need to get you dry and warmed up. Thanks to the previous tenants, even without electricity, upstairs we'll have light and heat of various sources. I might run every one of them, just to try to thaw out my feet."

Upon pulling off his gloves with his teeth, Gabe

dug into a pocket to find his penlight. A moment later, he and Hannah sighed in relief at the circle of light.

"How about yours?"

Hannah stomped her feet to knock off the snow that covered her shoes. "Cold, but not frozen." Slipping off her shoes, she headed for the store's back door and unlocked it.

"Where are you going? We need to get the pups and you upstairs next to some heat."

"I'm calling the phone hut to let someone know I'm all right."

With a grunt, Gabe quickly slipped off his own boots and followed her into the store. He swept the light ahead of Hannah as she headed for the counter and the cordless phone there.

In the glow of the flashlight, Gabe could see her frown of confusion when she picked up the receiver and lifted it to her ear. "It's dead."

With the beam, Gabe touched on the phone's base and the flat gray cord protruding from it. "The phone may be cordless, but it still uses electricity." As Hannah's face fell into more distress than he'd seen her express all the treacherous evening, Gabe put his arm around her. "The storm is supposed to stop by morning. They might have the power on before that, and we can call then. From what I know of the Amish, once the blowing stops, a little snow on the ground won't prevent them from getting around. In the meantime, let's get you and my wiggling passengers upstairs and warmed up. It's not bad down here right now, but without power and in this cold and wind, the temperature will drop fast. Come on."

He guided her to the back door. "Besides, I need

your help in figuring out how to get all this nonelectric stuff upstairs going."

Gabe had never been so thrilled to enter his apartment. With the help of Hannah and the penlight, kerosene lanterns left by the previous tenants were located and lit, along with the gas heater. By this time, the pups were ready to explore. Or something.

"Help," he murmured to Hannah when two cold noses poked under his chin and little tongues began licking his neck.

She came to his rescue, unzipping his coat and vest to collect the puppies. "They're hungry. I dropped the supplies just inside the door downstairs."

"I'll get it." Resurrecting his penlight from his pocket, Gabe slipped off his jump bag, set it next to the door and went on his errand. When he returned to the apartment, Hannah had her outer gear off and was on the floor by the heater with the pups in her lap.

He carried the supplies into the kitchen. "I've got a box in here from when I moved that will help keep them contained." He raised his voice so she could hear him in the other room. "I'm sure I could find a blanket to cushion it to sacrifice for the cause, as well."

"Sounds *gut*. How about a pan or bowl they can use for feeding?"

"I think I can dig something up."

Ten minutes later, he set a bowl of puppy food soaked in milk supplement on the floor. The pups scrambled over from their explorations of the room to eat. He and Hannah chuckled as one climbed into the bowl.

"Hey there, bud. You need to share with your sibling." Picking up the pup, Gabe set him outside the dish. While the puppies ate, their white-tipped tails wagging over their black backs, Hannah rose to her knees and inched her way closer to the heater.

"As the temperature drops, that'll feel even better."

"I don't think it could feel any better than it does right now," Hannah disagreed, holding her hands as close as possible to the emanating heat. She looked over when he knelt beside her. "You know I can't stay up here with you."

Gabe extended his fingers toward the heater. "I didn't risk our life and limb, or at least fingers and toes, to get you safely into town just to let you freeze downstairs. With the power off, there's no heat in the store." He stared at the red glow inside the heater. "If you're going to be stubborn about it, it would be better if you stayed up here and I went downstairs."

Hannah leaned over to poke him with her elbow. "*Ach*, were you always this contrary?"

"Me, contrary?" Gabe snorted. "I doubted my judgment and good sense in getting us out of the blizzard. And you're telling me you can't stay where it's safe and warm? If that's not the definition of contrary, I don't know what is."

They huddled in companionable silence, hands outstretched to the heater. Gabe swallowed audibly. "Another definition might be a woman who knows how much a man loves her, and knows she loves him, but won't agree to marry him."

For a moment, he didn't think she would respond. Was he wrong? Had he pushed too far? Memories of when he'd thought the same thing years before, only to have Hannah disappear, made Gabe feel colder than he had during their snowy walk into town.

"How about a man who pursues a woman when he knows the decision to marry him is…complicated?"

"I'm beginning to think he's just dense," Gabe muttered.

Hannah turned to smile at him. "I've wondered that a time or two myself."

Gabe tipped his little finger to tap against hers. "Should he give up hope?"

She hooked her pinkie around his. "If he can be patient just a little bit longer, there might be a chance."

Gabe shifted until they were touching shoulders. "He's a pretty patient guy."

For several heartbeats, there was only the sound of the flame inside the oil heater beside them and the occasional squeak of the puppies eating. When Hannah spoke again, it was barely above a whisper. "I'll… I'll talk to my parents when I see them again. And…tell Jethro that I can't marry him when I…love someone else."

Gabe's heart pounded enough he didn't need the heater to warm him. Drawing in a breath to respond, he grunted at the needle-sharp teeth that nipped his stockinged foot. Looking over his shoulder, he saw one of the pups had wandered from the bowl to find something else to nibble on. Scooping up the pup, he handed it to Hannah. "Since they're done, I'm going to fix some tea and something hot to eat on my gas stove so—" he looked intently at Hannah "—whoever goes downstairs is further fortified." Rising to his feet, Gabe headed for the kitchen.

"That will be *gut*," Hannah called to his back. "I'll appreciate that when I go downstairs."

Lighting the stove, Gabe snorted.

After the pups were settled and Hannah and Gabe had a meal of soup, tea and whatever else he could scrounge up, it was Hannah who went downstairs for the night. The debate continued as they descended the stairs by way of Gabe's penlight and another flashlight he'd unearthed. He refused to allow an oil or kerosene lamp down among the fabric.

"How do the *Englisch* manage to stay warm in the winter without electricity?" Hannah countered. "Surely they don't all freeze overnight?"

As he feared, the shop was already much cooler, even in the short time they'd been upstairs. "They probably have extra clothes to put on." Gabe considered it a victory that he'd finally persuaded Hannah to put on a pair of his socks. Her stockings were currently hanging on the back of a chair next to the heater to dry overnight. "Or extra blankets for the bed. You don't even have a bed. You'll be on the cold floor. Unless you think you're going to sleep on the countertop." He raised an eyebrow when a smile blossomed on Hannah's face.

"But I have blankets. Probably more than you do upstairs. I just need to get them down. And—" enthusiasm sparked her tone "—bags of batting would make a *wunderbar* mattress. I'll be more comfortable than you will."

When Gabe narrowed his eyes at her logic, Hannah lifted her light to expose all the quilts that lined the upper walls of the shop. He shook his head in reluctant admiration.

"Are you sure?" Gabe called as he fetched the chair by the counter. Sliding it next to the wall, he climbed upon it and started unclipping clothes pins that secured the quilts Hannah pointed out to him.

Hannah took the quilts as he handed them down. "Barb won't care. These are ones I made. In fact, she'd be helping me take them down if she was here."

"What would you have done if you'd worked in a grocery store? Used a bunch of soup cans for a mattress?"

Hannah carried her stack of quilts to the counter. "I'd have figured out something." They quickly made a bed on the floor beside the counter. Gabe had to admit when they were finished that it looked pretty comfy.

"Are you sure you don't want to stay upstairs where it might be warmer? I mean, I could stay here."

"*Nee*, I'll be fine."

"They'll probably have the electricity on by morning," Gabe said. "When you wake up, come upstairs for coffee, if not a little breakfast."

"Little being the key word."

He smiled at her teasing of his near-empty pantry. "I need to get back to the Bent 'N Dent and pick up some more expired breakfast bars." Gabe glanced at her face—this woman who'd endured so much with him tonight—shadowed in the indirect glow of their flashlights. "Well, good night. Call if you need anything. I mean call—" he cupped his hands about his mouth "—not call," he continued, nodding toward the inoperative phone.

"*Ja.*" Hannah held his gaze.

Even in the shadows, Gabe was pulled into the sweet warmth in her eyes. He felt himself lean in—an inch, two, three—before he froze.

With a long exhale, he shifted back. "Well, I probably better go. When did you say those two need to eat again?"

Hannah smiled, but was that disappointment he saw in the shadowy light? "In six hours."

With a brief nod, Gabe reluctantly backed toward the door. He didn't break eye contact until he bumped into the wall. "See you in the morning," he murmured. Her soft "good night" followed him out the door. Jubilant at having her close and at her earlier shy admission, the beam of his flashlight barely kept ahead of him as he took the stairs three at a time.

Hannah tucked the quilts about her. Snuggling more deeply into her nest, she grinned as she listened to the wind whine against the storefront glass and the corresponding creaks of the old building. The room temperature might be dropping, but she was cozy in her pallet. Directing the flashlight's beam to the ceiling overhead, she saw not the shadows it made on the painted surface, but the man in the apartment above it.

They'd been through so much tonight. It was hard to believe it was only a few hours since Gabe had offered to take her home. He'd trusted her to help with his emergency call and, later, she'd trusted him to keep them safe. They made a good team. If they could handle the challenges of the past few hours, surely together they could face any circumstances that would come their way?

She'd admitted she loved him. Hannah hugged the thought to herself. It felt good. The memory of what else she'd said—that she'd talk to her folks and Jethro—not so much. She flexed her fingers in their grip on the blankets. She needed to talk with the bishop, who was still recovering. Hannah's chest tightened with remorse.

She'd always done as she should. Surely just this once she could ignore the bishop's directive? Her parents had married for love, wouldn't they understand? And Jethro, the man had recently lost his wife. Surely any feelings he might have for Hannah were just simple respect at this point? *Gott* had created love and marriage, had he not? Surely he would understand a hope for love in the relationship? Hannah rearranged the batting she was using as a pillow. Her hope was for courage to face the upcoming confrontations.

Shifting to lie on her back, she winced at a poke into her hair. Touching her head, she rolled her eyes when she realized she still wore her prayer *kapp*. Sitting up, she unpinned it and set it on the counter. As she settled back down, her flashlight beam swept across the row of beige fabric that lined part of the aisle.

Redirecting the light onto the light brown material, Hannah recalled the events that'd occurred since Gabe had reentered her life. Saving the bishop, initiating a community project, confronting the man she now knew was Mr. Weathers, helping and forgiving him tonight, rescuing puppies and trudging through a snowstorm to name a few. Maybe she wasn't a drab beige after all. While she might not be the rich blue Gabe saw her as, Hannah mused, drifting off to sleep, perhaps she was at least a green hue.

Blinking open her eyes in the feeble morning light, Hannah found herself in a canyon. It took a moment to recognize its fabric walls. Snuggling into her blan-

ket cocoon, the events of the previous evening came
back to her. The accident. The storm. The treacherous
walk into town. Gabe. Upstairs. The lack of electricity to call her folks.

Even as Hannah acknowledged her cold nose, com-
pliments of the room's low temperature, a low hum
rumbled throughout it. The shop's furnace was kicking
on. Ceiling lights she'd forgotten to turn off when she'd
abruptly left last night flickered before fully illuminat-
ing the area. Hannah smiled. Lights, heat, the phone.

The phone! Scrambling out of her nest, she snatched
the receiver off its cradle on the counter. Sighing in
relief at the dial tone, she tapped out the number to
the phone hut nearest to her farm and left a breathless
message for her folks.

Mission accomplished, she pulled a quilt off her
makeshift bed to wrap about her. Hannah searched for
her shoes before remembering she'd taken them upstairs to dry out next to Gabe's heater. Gabe's heater,
which would have kept the apartment reasonably
warm. At least warmer than this.

Would Gabe be awake yet? Never having been at
the shop this time of day, she didn't know when he
got around. Hannah smiled. The pups would probably change his schedule this morning. Tipping her
head, Hannah listened for any sounds from the apartment upstairs, but the growl of the furnace drowned
out anything else.

He'd mentioned coffee. And she needed her shoes.
Surely if she was quiet, it might be possible to ob-
tain both without bothering him? Besides, she wanted
to check on the pups. But if Gabe was already up, it

would be the first breakfast she'd have with him. That their first of many shared breakfasts might start with expired breakfast bars expanded Hannah's smile.

The need for warmth, coffee and Gabe was superseded by the habit of setting the shop to rights first. Hannah bustled about, gathering and carefully folding the quilts to rehang later. When all looked as it should be, she headed for the back door. Her first steps on the stairs were hesitant, until she heard the tread of someone moving about above her; then she fairly skipped up the stairway.

"Morning." Gabe gestured her into the apartment with the coffee cup he held.

"Good morning." Hannah couldn't stop the flush that bloomed on her cheeks as she entered. Although Gabe was dressed, his light brown hair was tousled. She'd never seen him before with as much stubble on his cheeks.

"Can I get you some?" He lifted his cup again.

"*Ja.* Please." Instead of following him into the kitchen, she checked on the status of their young charges. The pups were curled up, asleep in the blanketed box.

Gabe reemerged and handed her a cup. "They were fed again just a bit ago. They're…quite effective in making their needs known." He tipped his head toward the lamp emitting a dim glow near the sofa. "Power's on. County should be digging out soon. Did you get your call made?"

"*Ja.* Left a message. Someone should pick it up soon. I just couldn't stand to have them worry."

"I understand. Thankfully I didn't get paged last night, but I need to get another cell phone lined up. And get someone to pull my truck out of the ditch.

Hopefully it's still sitting upright. But first, breakfast. Do you want a breakfast bar, or a breakfast bar?"

"Hmm. That's a difficult decision. I think I'll have a breakfast bar."

"Good choice." Gabe disappeared into the kitchen again, brought out two bars and handed one to Hannah. They ate them standing over the heater.

Upon finishing, Hannah gathered up her stockings and shoes from where they'd been set to dry. "I need to go back downstairs. I came to check on the pups and to get my shoes."

Gabe wadded up his wrapper. "Not for my fantastic breakfast?"

Hannah smiled. "Well, that, too. But I…shouldn't be up here alone with you."

Gabe sighed, but his intent gaze reminded Hannah of her agreement last night to talk with the bishop and her family about her relationship with him.

Snagging her outer gear from the pegs near the door, Gabe gestured for Hannah to precede him downstairs. "I'll go down with you to use the phone. I need to leave messages at work and the tow service." Both of them in stocking feet, their treads were quiet on the stairs.

"While I wait, I might wander out to see if the truck's okay. Maybe I'll take a shovel with me, to try to dig it out. And then I might go to where the accident was. Maybe root around in the snow a bit like a St. Bernard and try to find my phone."

Hannah giggled at the image of Gabe pawing in the ditch, snow flying out behind him. "Watching you do that would almost be worth the walk out to the truck."

"Store won't open for a while. You're welcome to join me…"

Gabe held the shop's door open for her. Basking in his smile, Hannah grinned up at him and walked through under his arm. A motion at the shop's wide windows drew her attention. Three men were looking into the shop, a team of draft horses and sleigh behind them. Hannah's breath caught with joy at seeing her father and two oldest brothers. Until she watched the transition from shock to dismay on Zebulun Lapp's face before his expression morphed into somber lines.

Through the glass, Hannah saw his gaze shift from her to Gabe and back again. Glancing at Gabe, unshaven with rumbled hair, his arm at the door practically around her, Hannah then looked down at her wrinkled dress. She instantly knew what her father was thinking.

Zebulun Lapp's attention lingered above her frozen stare. Reaching up with her free hand, Hannah patted her head, gasping when her fingers touched only mussed hair. Her glance flew to the counter where her *kapp* sat where she'd put it last night. Dropping her shoes and stockings, Hannah dashed over, snatched up her prayer covering and pulled it into position, her fingers fumbling to gather the pins from the counter's slick surface.

When she looked outside again, her father was turning away from the window. Racing to the door, Hannah quickly unlocked it and ran outside. *"Daed!"*

Her father turned, his gaze sweeping from the hastily positioned *kapp* to her feet, clad in Gabe's socks, on the snow covered sidewalk. He sighed. "Your *mamm* and I worried about you when you didn't come home. We wanted to make sure you were all right."

Hannah didn't feel the cold of the snow under her feet or the frigid breeze through the thin material of her dress. She was too hot with shame. "I'm so sorry. I helped Gabe with an accident last night. I was going to call but the power went out and he lost his phone in the snow." Even to her ears, it sounded far-fetched. "I left a message this morning at the phone hut. I spent the night downstairs in the shop. Truly."

Her *daed*'s gaze lifted to above and behind her. Hannah felt a weight settle over her shoulders and discovered Gabe had covered her with her cloak. Zebulun turned his attention to the draft horses who were stomping their feet in the snow. "I need to let your *mamm* know I found you. Do you need anything before I go?"

I need to know that you're not upset with me. That you don't think I've let you down. That I haven't brought shame upon you. Hannah almost sobbed the words. She'd lived her life striving to always do the right thing. Responding to everything with humble obedience. Except for the times when she first met and secretly went out with Gabe. With a twist in her stomach, she watched her *daed* climb into the sleigh. "Where are you going?"

Zebulun settled onto the bench seat, Hannah's brothers climbed silently into the sleigh beside him. "Your *mamm* wants some groceries since we're in town. And when the feed store opens, I need some minerals for the cows."

"I'll go with you!"

With a look at her feet, Zebulun frowned. "You'll need shoes."

"Just give me a moment, please!" Hannah turned, almost bumping into Gabe as she dashed into the shop. He followed more slowly behind her, standing a few feet away as she jerked off his socks and struggled to put on her air-dried stockings while standing on one foot.

"Hannah."

She set her foot down on the cold floor, stocking bunched at the heel, and clamped her hands to her cheeks. "I can't, Gabe. I'm sorry. I thought I could marry you. But to do so would hurt my family. I can't… I can't bear to shame them like I just did."

"But we didn't do anything…"

"We did. *I* did. I saw his face. I hurt my *daed*. It was something I promised myself I'd never do after seeing the pain and shame they felt when Gail left."

Hannah couldn't see him clearly through her tear-blurred vision. "I need to do as my parents wish. To follow *Gott*'s will as the bishop wishes and…and marry elsewhere." Kneeling, she finished pulling on her stockings and slid her feet into clammy shoes. The laces were too stiff to hurry, so Hannah drew in a few deep breaths as she clumsily tied them. As she straightened to stand, she brushed the tears from her face. She almost sobbed anew at Gabe's expression. Even the man in the wreck last night hadn't looked as defeated.

"I'm sorry," she whispered before turning for the door. As she went through, she locked it. At the heavy click on the old door, Hannah couldn't help but think she was locking up something else, as well.

Her heart.

Chapter Sixteen

Wisconsinites were experts in digging out after winter storms. Within a day, the town was set to rights. Within two days, other than deeper drifts in ditches and across fields, it was as if the storm had never happened.

But Hannah knew better. She pushed peas around her plate with her fork, dodging other uneaten food from The Dew Drop's daily special. In those two days, she hadn't had the courage to talk with her *daed*. It wasn't that they'd been avoiding each other. When Hannah was home, her *daed* had been busy with extra chores due to the storm. At supper, with her folks and her four *brieder* interacting around the table, her subdued silence wasn't noticeable.

Unlike here. Hannah glanced up to find Jethro watching her while he ate. Feeling her cheeks heat, she dropped her gaze again to her plate and set down her fork. Ruby Weaver had stopped by the shop late yesterday, ostensibly to buy fabric to finish binding her quilt. Hannah recognized the visit as judgment to see if she was chastened enough to still be a worthy wife for the bishop's son.

Right now, she didn't feel worthy of anyone. Hannah squeezed her eyes shut at the knowledge of the pain she'd caused Gabe. Of how fickle he must think her. She knew she loved him. But she'd learned from when she was just beyond a *boppeli* how vital *gelassenheit* was to Amish society. Yielding to the will of *Gott* and others was woven into the fabric of their lives. The welfare of the community was more important than individual rights and choices. More important than her choice. Gabe. Who could never be more than just an aching dream or memory to Hannah.

Opening her eyes, she slid her napkin over to wipe away a teardrop from the table's glossy surface. Jethro Weaver was a good man. It was time she focused on reality and not wishes, hopes and dreams. This was her future, if he'd still have her. This man. Whom she needed to get to know.

A concept easier said than done without a conversation. So far, she'd asked how the bishop was doing after his incident. "Fine" had been the reply, with no elaboration. Had Jethro had any problems with the storm? "No." After numerous other one-word answers, she'd left the man to eat his roast beef and potatoes in peace.

Hannah glanced around the restaurant, unintentionally catching Mrs. Edigers's eye. The midwife smiled and waved from where she was eating with her husband. Hannah nodded back, feeling a flash of joy at the memory of working with the woman to bring Ruth's baby into the world. Her expression softened at the reminder of the amazement of *Gott*'s creation, the wonder of birth and the opportunity to help mothers through the anxious time of delivery. Hannah had a great deal of respect and admiration for what the older woman did.

Her attention returned to her dinner companion. Jethro's silence gave her a lot of time to think. That could be a good thing. Or—Hannah's mouth grew dry as she watched someone approach the door through the restaurant's windows—a bad thing.

Appetite now completely gone, Hannah nudged her plate away. She watched Gabe stop outside the restaurant door to stomp snow from his feet. Reaching for the door handle, he glanced inside. And froze when his gaze connected with hers. Hannah sucked in a breath when he pivoted and walked back down the street. She was still watching when he turned the corner.

Mouth quivering, Hannah was concentrating on folding her napkin for the third time when she thought she heard words from across the table.

"How's the f-fundraiser going?"

She'd have been less shocked to hear Daisy ask a question during the drive home. Eyes wide, Hannah stared at her dinner companion.

Jethro raised an eyebrow. "The f-fundraiser?" he prompted.

"Uh, *ja*. I—I don't know if it's going to happen." Hannah pulled the napkin into her lap and proceeded to unfold it.

Jethro raised his other eyebrow.

Hannah interpreted that as asking why. She took a quick sip of water. "Uh, there doesn't seem to be much support for it anymore. Interest was lost when Aaron

Raber left. And maybe more after the storm when I… I don't know if I'll continue to pursue it." Setting the glass down, she traced its condensation ring on the wooden table. Surely the man knew his mother was the primary one stifling the project.

When she glanced up, Jethro was watching her as he picked up the last roll from the basket and buttered it. Hannah hunched a shoulder at his continued attention. "Something else will come up to raise the funds." She sighed. "The *Englisch* will probably do something. Someone might write another grant. The community will get local EMS service eventually."

"Eventually," he echoed, breaking the bread into smaller pieces. "T-takes t-time."

"Ja," Hannah murmured. Time that Gabe didn't have. She cleared her throat. "It won't be this particular person. But the community will get the help it needs at some point. Isn't that the important part?" She tried to smile when meeting Jethro's thoughtful gaze, but her lips kept trembling. Retrieving her napkin, she held it against her mouth until her lips were as firm as she knew her resolve needed to be.

Jethro nodded slowly, his eyes solemn. "F-finished?"

Nodding in return, Hannah stood. Yes, with anything to do with Gabe, she needed to be finished.

Gabe trudged up the stairs to his apartment, his legs heavy with the same lead that filled his stomach. If he'd needed proof that it was over between him and Hannah, he'd just had it. Shoving open the door, the first thing he saw when he looked into the room were the blue curtains at the window. He crossed the room to touch the rich fabric.

"It's curtains for me," he murmured as he leaned against the wall. It certainly was. It was the end of any hopes he might have of a future with Hannah. The end of his job here in town. Gabe snorted. He'd learned that bit when he'd called the office as soon as he'd replaced his phone. The administrator had heard the fundraiser was off. With no source of funds in sight, there was no choice but to terminate the position. As the budget was already running in the red, Gabe would be paid for what he'd already worked, but surely he could understand...

Gabe could understand all right. As of this weekend, he had no reason, either personally or professionally, to stay in Miller's Creek. Too bad he'd already unpacked and disposed of the boxes.

Except for one. At the squeaks generating from a large carton, Gabe ambled over to squat down and regard its two occupants. Upon blinking their eyes open, the pups waddled over to greet him. Gabe ran a few fingers over their silky heads. Trying to reach him, they scratched with tiny paws up the side of the box. Scooping a pup in each hand, Gabe returned to the window and settled on the floor next to it with his back against the wall.

"Well, kiddos." He set the pups on his lap. "If I love her, like I say I do, I want her to be happy." He sighed. "Something I thought involved me being in her life. But what makes her happy is being connected with her family and community. And I complicate that. Maybe it's a good thing the job fell through." Gabe smiled ruefully as both pups put their paws on his chest and began licking his chin. "Because I can't stay here and see her married to another man. I...I just can't."

He shifted the pups back to his lap. "But when we go, we're taking these curtains with us. We'll put them up in our next place. That all right with you guys? 'Cause you're going with me. You're part of my family now." Gabe ran a hand down their fuzzy black backs. They felt so warm and vibrant, when he couldn't recall being so cold, even in the midst of the blizzard.

The men were getting up from the tables, which, with much practice, had been hastily arranged after the church service. Hannah was refilling the water pitchers for the next seating while other women were clearing up from the previous one or preparing more food.

With a squeak, Hannah hastily shut off the faucet and drained some excess water from the pitcher. *Gut* thing she wasn't pouring coffee today. Her mind wasn't anywhere near her task. It was where it'd been the past four days since she last saw him. On Gabe. On the ache in her stomach, knowing she'd never see him again. She'd heard he was leaving. And why wouldn't he? She'd chosen family and community over him. Again.

Hannah dodged through the traffic on the way to the tables, her expression grim. Maybe it was understandable that some couples were content to start their marriages with just respect. It was less unsettling than love. Hannah caught her mother's frown of concern as Willa grabbed a cloth to wipe up the water that'd just sloshed over the rim of Hannah's pitcher. Head lowered, Hannah continued to the table and began filling glasses.

Surely she could be happy without Gabe? She'd spent years without him, years when she'd been… beige. Hannah bit the inside of her cheek. Beige wasn't bad. It just wasn't…blue. But maybe blue wasn't for her. At the end of a row, Hannah turned her back to the room, pulled the pitcher to her chest and lowered her head. *Dear Gott, I trust in Your will. Help me to respect your chosen one for me and teach me to love him even a small measure of the way I love…someone else.*

Draining what remained in the pitcher into the next glass with tear-bleared eyes, Hannah pivoted to return to the kitchen, before halting abruptly in the middle of the room. Jethro stood before her, eyes on her face. He cleared his throat. His face was so red, the white scar above his lip stood out in sharp relief.

"Hannah L-Lapp." Hannah flinched at the unexpected volume of his voice. It was abnormally pitched to draw attention. Glancing around, she saw if that had been his intent, he'd succeeded immensely. All heads were turned in their direction. Her cheeks heated as her own color began to rise.

"I have s-something I n-need to ask you."

Chapter Seventeen

❧

Pinning a faltering smile on her face, Hannah braced for what Jethro might say next. Even though she knew it was what the bishop willed, inwardly, she cringed. *Please don't let him declare himself here. Please don't let him ask to walk out with me in front of the whole community. I know my duty is to marry him, but please don't let it start out like this.*

This action seemed so out of character for taciturn Jethro, but then again, did she really know him, this man who was to be her husband, at all?

"I have some b-b-birdhouses and a b-b-bushel." He closed his eyes in frustration of getting the words out. This was obviously as painful for him as it was for Hannah. *So why was he doing it?* "Of walnuts. F-for the auction. Where d-do you want them? You're still organizing that, right? Is the d-date for it still the same?"

Hannah's jaw sagged. She'd been braced for a question, but not this one. Should she go on with the auction? This man, who might become her husband, thought she should. And with a quick search of her heart, Hannah knew it was the right decision. Recovering from her shock, she was sorely tempted to throw her arms around the man. Reaching out the hand not holding the pitcher, she grasped his work-calloused fingers. "Oh *denki*, Jethro, *denki*," she whispered for his ears alone.

Dropping his hand as quickly as she'd grabbed it, she cleared her throat and spoke at his previous emphatic volume. "*Ja*. It's still on. The date is the same. *Denki* for the *wunderbar* contributions. If folks aren't able to bring items the day of the auction, I… I'll collect them at our farm."

Jethro nodded stiffly, something closely resembling a smile on his normally solemn face. *"Gut."* Was that almost a twinkle in his eyes?

Hannah swallowed hard as she watched him pivot and rejoin a group of men, who along with all others in the room, were curiously observing the interaction. The expressions on the surrounding faces were intrigued. Positive. Supportive? Just as Jethro had probably anticipated when he'd fairly leaped out of his comfort zone to offer his support. The man who had the most to lose if she succeeded in keeping Gabe in town had just revitalized the project that could keep him there.

Hannah felt… She didn't know what she felt.

She'd just asked *Gott* to help her love the man she would marry. Was this the beginning of His plan? She'd respected Jethro, or what she'd known of him from her minimal acquaintance, but his actions today showed her more of his qualities.

She may never feel for him the way she did about Gabe, but this solemn man certainly now had her admiration. Surely love could grow from that? Hannah had seen relationships develop into good marriages that had started with less.

Gott was answering her prayer. Showing her how to love another man. The revelation was reason to be elated. But if this was elation, why was she so close to crying?

Hannah was concentrating on blinking back threatening tears when Samuel Schrock kept her the center of attention, calling out, "Hannah, I'll be bringing a horse to the auction. I suppose you'd rather I keep him at home until that day rather than leave him on your porch?" Her brother-in-law's comment drew chuckles from around the room.

"Is that the one that's blind in one eye and has three lame legs?" Someone wasted no time in teasing the local horse trader.

"*Nee*, Freeman Hershberger, I sold that one to you for a hefty profit." The chuckles grew to outright laughs.

Hannah started when someone touched her on the arm. Susannah Mast, Rachel and Rebecca's mother, smiled as she took the pitcher from Hannah's hands. "That reminds me, I have several jars of honey and some goat milk soap I'll be bringing to the auction. Would it be helpful if I just brought them straight in that day? I'll be there. Especially now that I know Jethro is bringing in walnuts. Although—" raising her voice, Susannah turned toward the women still working in the kitchen "—I'll probably have to bid against Naomi for them."

One of the older women drying dishes responded with a nod of her head. "*Ach*, for certain you will. But at least I know what to do with them once I bring them home."

"You may be right," quipped Susannah over the corresponding giggles. "I've never been known for my baking. Maybe I'll just go for one of the birdhouses." With a hand on Hannah's shoulder, she led her into the kitchen. While some women still hung back, watching dubiously, the pair was stopped by a procession of others, advising Hannah on what they planned to bring to the auction and asking further questions about the project.

By the time everyone had eaten and the dishes were done, Hannah had lost track of all the items being donated and the people who'd assured her they'd be at the auction. Overwhelmed by the abrupt shift of the day and needing a moment to herself during a lull, Hannah grabbed a chore jacket from a peg on the wall and slipped out the back door. Sliding her arms into the oversize sleeves, she was enveloped with the familiar scents of hay and livestock. Knowing the men would be congregating in the barn to visit, she headed instead to a side yard, her objective a picnic table beyond the clothesline that stretched over the snow-tramped ground.

Brushing the snow from the wooden seat, she sank down onto it, tucking the encompassing jacket under her. Although there'd been a few frowns and suspicious gazes, Hannah was humbled by the outpouring of support. Tipping back her head, she considered the winter blue sky overhead. This is why she loved the Plain community. This is why she needed to stay. They took care of each other. Beyond love and obedience to *Gott*, the bands of family, friendship and unity were the foundation of the community.

She squeezed her eyes tight against the prickle of tears. One escaped to slip down her temple into her hairline. If she married Gabe, she'd miss that. Would she eventually resent him for pulling her away? Could she adjust to their new existence? Who would be their community? Her role in the Plain world was so much a part of her identity. Hannah knew her place in it. At least, she knew who she was supposed to be in it. Who would she be without it?

Hannah's lips trembled. She stilled them with chilled fingers.

Oh, but those happy few days with Gabe before Aaron Raber left, when the community had buzzed with gratitude that Bishop Weaver had been saved and it seemed anything was possible.

To the surprise and delight of the congregation, Bishop Weaver was in attendance today. He didn't preach, but had remained seated in the one upholstered chair remaining in the room. She'd caught him watching her speculatively a few times. If he had an opinion on the auction, Hannah hadn't spoken with anyone who'd heard it.

She smiled faintly. She might think one thing in regard to interactions with her future mother-in-law. But whenever she thought of her future father-in-law, she'd be thinking of the man who'd shown her how to save Bishop Weaver's life. Noticeably absent today in expressing any support was Ruby Weaver. If Hannah had caught the bishop's eyes on her, his wife's gaze had seemed to burn a hole through Hannah's *kapp*. She and Gabe may have saved her husband's heart, but the action certainly hadn't warmed his wife's any.

Hannah tried to shrug off her dismay. She'd find a way of making a marriage with Jethro work. She had to. Still, the prospect of being daughter-in-law to Ruby Weaver filled her mouth with the taste of milk gone sour.

But, she drew in a long breath, feeling the cold air as it raced through her nose, it was apparently *Gott*'s plan.

The soft crunching of feet on snow announced someone's presence in the yard. Shifting on the bench, Hannah turned to see her *mamm* crossing the yard. Willa Lapp wore a gentle smile as she approached.

"Is this a private gathering?"

"There's always room for you, *Mamm*." Hannah brushed snow off the seat beside her.

Tucking her black cloak about her, Willa sat. "Sounds like your auction will be a success."

"*Ach*, it's not my auction. But if *Gott* wills it, I certainly hope so. I'll work to make it so." Hannah's voice dropped to a whisper. "It seems it's also His will that I marry Jethro."

Willa nodded. "Jethro is a *gut* man." She put her hand over where Hannah's rested in her lap. "But what is your will?"

Hannah looked at her *mamm* in surprise. "My will doesn't matter. *Gelassenheit* is abandoning my will in favor of following divine will, as Christ has done."

"*Ja*. That is so. You will think me a poor influence today. It's wrong to be *hochmut* as well, but I am so proud of the way you have obeyed throughout your life. I couldn't have asked for a better *dochder*. And now, because I am your *mamm* and love you, I have a question for you. Does the thought of marrying Jethro make you happy?"

She apparently had her answer when Hannah's eyes filled with tears. Willa squeezed her hand. "I rejoice and give thanks to *Gott* that your sister was returned to us. I rejoice more that she is happy. Have you ever wondered if marriage to Jethro is *Gott*'s will, or the bishop's?"

Hannah's eyes widened. "Wouldn't the bishop be implementing *Gott*'s will?"

Her *mamm* smiled. "We would like to think so. And sometimes it is so. But we are all still human and can be selfish in different ways." Her smile ebbed and her eyes softened with compassion. "Large families are a blessing from *Gott*. Bishop Weaver and his wife have suffered many losses. Jethro is their only living child. They want to see him settled with a family of his own. Perhaps the bishop is a bit biased on what he sees as *Gott*'s will, in this case. According to James in the *Biewel*, wisdom from above is many things, including impartial.

"Besides, sometimes *Gott* softly whispers his instructions instead of shouting them from the hayloft. Pray that your heart and mind are open to the subtlety of his direction. His ways are mysterious."

Pausing, Willa sighed. "Jethro recently lost his wife and unborn child. Our faith believes it isn't right to grieve overmuch when a loved one dies, as that is to question *Gott*'s will. I'm sure Jethro wants to be a *gut* son to his parents and do as they wish, but it might be soon for him to be thinking of marrying again. Has he given you any reason to believe he wants this match as much as his parents do?"

Thinking back over the painfully silent meals with Jethro, Hannah realized he'd never given an indication he was interested in a match between them. So why the public support of the auction today? Was it an effort to tilt her toward Gabe and away from himself? Her heart rate accelerated at the possibility.

"If I'd married the man my bishop wanted me to, I'd be in Indiana working in a nursery now. I like animals better than plants. I guess I'd rather help make the fertilizer than sell it."

Hannah's jaw dropped at her *mamm*'s admission.

"The bishop wanted me to marry his nephew. It took me prompting, sometimes subtly, sometimes not so subtly, to get Zebulun Lapp to give me a ride home from a singing before the bishop's choice could ask me. I've never regretted it. The way *Gott* has blessed me since, if following my heart was wrong, He has more than forgiven me, He has blessed me abundantly indeed."

"Mamm!" They shared an amused glance.

"Your *daed* still takes a little bit of prompting now and then. He loves you and is also proud of you, even though he isn't one for saying it. *Ja*, he was surprised the other day. We were desperately worried about you. Your *daed*'s reaction was more his version of relief than of judgment."

"He looked so disheartened. And when Gail left…"

Her *mamm* reached out to wipe tears Hannah wasn't aware of running down her cheek. "The reason we were so upset when Abigail left is that we were worried about her surviving in the *Englisch* world. Not for whatever was happening to us in the community. *Ja*, there was gossip—" Willa raised an eyebrow "—which *Gott* says is a sin, as well. But not from the ones who matter to us, and there were many of those. And Gail is not you. She's a little more…impetuous." Willa lowered her hands to gently encase Hannah's clenched ones. "Sometimes you think too much."

After a light squeeze, her *mamm* released Hannah's

hands. "Gabriel Bartel seems like a *gut* man. He must be, or my *dochder* wouldn't care for him so. Your *daed* and I will survive whatever you decide to do. And, as long as you make your choice prior to baptism, you will not truly leave us. Only members baptized into the church risk being shunned.

"Marriage is for life. I milk cows twice a day for three hundred and sixty-five days, because I like who I'm doing it with. You will sit across from your husband for breakfast and supper every day. For many years. If the face across the table isn't dear to you, those years can be very lonely."

They both turned their heads when a voice called her *mamm*'s name. Hannah's *daed* stood at the yard's white fence. "Willa, the cows are waiting on us. The older boys are staying for the singing." Hannah inhaled sharply when he turned his attention to her. It hitched further when his normally reserved expression eased into a gentle smile. "Will you be staying, as well?"

Hannah wanted to leap from the bench and race to her *daed* for a hug. Although her legs tensed for activity, she remained seated, knowing the action would embarrass them both. Just his smile of acceptance was enough to know she was loved. Besides, she had much to think about. For the moment, the quiet yard seemed a good place in which to do so. Sharing her father's smile, she gave a hesitant nod.

Pushing to her feet, Willa brushed the snow from the back of her black cloak. Zebulun Lapp opened the gate and extended a hand to help his wife over an icy patch. Hannah barely heard her *daed*'s words and her *mamm*'s reply.

"Like a singing long ago, I'll be with the prettiest girl in the room."

"I must've aged well then. I've progressed to the prettiest one in the barn. I think *Gott* will forgive me for being *hochmut* that I'm better looking than a herd of Holsteins."

Watching them leave, Hannah's heart warmed at their obvious devotion so many years into marriage. It was the relationship she'd hoped for. One she knew she could have…with Gabe. She mulled over her *mamm*'s words. Over the events of the afternoon. Had not *Gott* renewed the possibility of the fundraiser? And with it, the possibility of Gabe staying? Had not *Gott* had Gabe show Hannah how to do CPR, and because of that knowledge, they'd been able to save the bishop's life? Which in turn had earned latent goodwill for Gabe in the community and displayed the need for the EMS service? And the storm, and the accident? If not for them, nothing would have changed and she'd have remained floundering in her decision, or lack thereof. What else might *Gott* be whispering, if she'd only listen?

Had she herself asked what path *Gott* wanted for her, or had she just assumed others knew best? Hannah pressed her lips together. Much was lost for want of asking. Her breathing shallow, she bowed her head.

"*Gott*, please help me to do Your will. Help me to be open to know what it is. Direct me to Your path forward." Hannah stared unseeing at the snowy yard beyond her seat. Even motionless, her heart was racing and her breathing shallow. She closed her eyes. "*Gott*, if there is any way that Your will for me could include Gabe, please shout it from the hayloft, as I certainly don't want to risk missing Your gentle whisper on that. Because…because that would be my choice."

Opening her eyes with a deep exhalation, she rose from the wooden seat. Hannah paused when two men, one coming from the house, the other from the direction of the barn, stopped to talk in the middle of the farmyard. From the looks Bishop Weaver and Jethro sent her at interludes, a tight feeling in her stomach told Hannah the discussion involved her.

After a moment, Bishop Weaver turned and headed back to the house, leaving his son in the middle of the farmyard. Jethro hesitated, casting a longing look toward the field where his rig was parked, before heading for the yard gate. Shutting it behind him, he crunched through the snow to where Hannah stood.

He stopped a short distance away, his expression solemn. When he didn't immediately speak, Hannah shifted, feeling the cold seep through her feet for the first time since she'd come out.

Jethro sighed. "Hannah. You are a f-fine woman. I know you will m-make a *g-gut* wife. B-but not for m-me right now." He frowned. "It's t-too soon after…"

Hannah held up her hand, sparing him further words as excitement grew within her. This sounded like more than a whisper. "It's all right. I understand."

Seeming encouraged by her response, he continued. "I understand if you are n-not available after some t-time p-passes." A smile rose, more in his eyes than in the slight curve of his mouth. "I'll l-look around. See if I can f-find more things f-for the auction. I think this auction w-will be successful f-for you. That it will b-bring in everything you hope."

Hannah's eyes widened. Was the cancelation of this relationship *Gott*'s endorsement for another?

Nodding, Jethro left the yard, with a lighter step than when he'd come in, but no more buoyant than Hannah's as she dashed for the house.

She flew in the back door, her heart thumping in her chest. Hanging the borrowed coat on a nearby peg, she felt eyes on her. Turning, Hannah found Bishop Weaver in the mudroom, his frown accented by the ravages of his recent illness on his gaunt face.

"Hannah Lapp. I…"

Hannah stood tensely as the bishop studied her, her heart in her throat. Hadn't *Gott* been displaying His will? And it matched hers, not the bishop's. Hoping she wasn't going to provoke the man into another heart attack, Hannah opened her mouth to tell him so.

Bishop Weaver spoke first. "Martha Edigers came to talk with me in the hospital. She said it's time for her to think about retirement. She knows our community needs a midwife. There's not a large population of Mennonites in the area, but they've always gotten on well with Plain folks. But none of her people are interested." His gaze pinned Hannah as he frowned. "She said you have the touch. She said if you wanted to apprentice with her, she would work with you to become certified." His brows lowered as if Hannah had challenged him. "You do understand that something else might need to be arranged while you have young children."

Hannah held her breath as she waited for his next words. Surely *Gott* was raising His voice to the barn rafters? If she was allowed, no, instructed to take more training for the community, a rarity for an Amish woman, perhaps she wasn't to stay in the church?

The bishop swallowed, his rawboned throat bobbing. "I have some hens that haven't been laying well. No sense in feeding them if they're not earning their keep. They'd make *gut* fryers for someone. I will have them there for the auction. I…I hope it's a success and…and will get you what you want. It's…it's *gut* to have such fast medical care in the district."

Bishop Weaver's unblinking eyes, huge in his thin face, studied Hannah. "Will you be staying in the community with this Mennonite man?"

Hannah's heart was pounding. "If he'll have me." Her palms sweating, she straightened her shoulders and met his intent gaze.

"All right then. I will inform Mrs. Edigers that you will be contacting her about the apprenticeship."

Grabbing her cloak and bonnet, Hannah nodded hastily to those remaining in the house as she hurried outside. She skidded to a halt at the end of the sidewalk. Her parents had left, and she had no transportation. But she had brothers and a brother-in-law in the barn who did. She started picking her way over the frozen rutted ground of the farmyard.

Jethro was driving his rig out from the field where church attendees had been parked. He pulled alongside her. "D-do you need a r-ride into t-town?"

"Ja. Denki." Hannah scrambled into the buggy beside her previous suitor. "Is your horse fast?"

Jethro gathered the reins. "I hope so. I b-bought him from your b-brother-in-law."

Bursting through the alley door into the hallway, Hannah dashed up the narrow stairs two at a time. Her haste reminded her of her actions a few weeks ago. Then, to revive a friend. Now, to hopefully resuscitate a relationship. When Gabe opened the door to her knock, this time it was his face that displayed shock at who was on the other side.

"Hannah! What are you doing here?" He scanned beyond her. "Are you here alone?"

"*Ja* and *nee.* There's no one else with me. But, Gabe, I hope I'm no longer alone. I hope there's still a chance to be with you. As your wife. Jethro is donating things for the auction and doesn't want to marry yet, and Samuel has a horse he's offering and many others have things they'll be contributing. Even Bishop Weaver is bringing chickens and he needs me to become Mrs. Edigers for the community. It is so *wunderbar*!"

His gentle hands gripped her upper arms. "Slow down. You lost me at chickens."

"That's what's *wunderbar*! I thought I'd lost you forever but *Gott* showed me His will through chickens and my *mamm* not marrying the bishop's nephew and an apprenticeship that I'm not forgoing His will to marry you. In fact, I'm following it…" Hannah took in Gabe's round-eyed look. Glancing through the apartment's open door, she noticed the boxes. Boxes for him to move away. Her gaze returned to Gabe's green eyes and she took a deep breath. "If you'll have me. Will you?"

Just like before, he tugged her into his arms. Hannah went willingly, holding on to him with all her strength.

"I thought you'd never ask," he murmured before he kissed her.

Epilogue

Hannah turned from paying the auctioneer, her smile as wide as the man's trailer. Even so, it managed to expand even farther when she caught sight of Gabe weaving his way through the thinning crowd.

She gestured with the record book and fat manila envelope in her hand. "Looks like you'll be here a little longer."

His smiling green eyes held hers as he crossed the last few feet. "Good thing, as I'm getting married next Thursday."

Hannah's cheeks flushed. She still was amazed that she'd soon become Gabe's wife. "You must be a risk-taker."

"I had faith. In God, and the person arranging the fundraiser." He winked at her. "And I'd have figured out a backup plan. Much is lost for want of asking, you know."

"So I've heard. Since you haven't asked, I'll tell you that we raised enough to fund the EMS program for the next year. Even maybe expand it so my husband isn't always on call by himself. And perhaps next year, a used service vehicle, if he has the contacts to find one." Gabe's eyes widened and his mouth dropped open. Before he got too excited, Hannah cautioned, "A bargain one."

"Bargains are always good." He smiled wryly. "Particularly with Nip and Tuck growing so much they're eating me out of house and home. When the time comes, I'll certainly explore my resources. And now we know a decent mechanic, as Clay Weathers is working on opening his business again." Taking her free hand, Gabe led her away from the trailer. "In the crowd today, if I heard it once, I heard it ten times— come next year… You've started something amazing. I can't thank you enough for making this possible."

"*Gott* made this possible."

"I can't thank Him enough. Mainly for you."

Hannah felt the same. Her heart was full. The blue dress she'd made for her wedding was hanging in her room. Hannah touched it every night just to remind herself what seemed impossible would soon become real.

Granted, their wedding would be a more subdued event than a normal one in the Plain community. But those who counted would still be there. Because she was marrying outside the faith, she couldn't join the church—which hurt—but she could still interact in the community. As evidenced by support of the auction, she was still accepted by most of the Amish district. And it was early yet. She'd just started apprenticing with Mrs. Edigers. Folks were more relieved they'd continue to have a midwife when the elderly Mennonite woman retired than concerned that a fellow Amish woman was marrying a Mennonite man.

Ja, she had much to thank *Gott* for.

"I don't know how you finished this in time." Gabe's comment drew Hannah's attention to the folded quilt sitting on a nearby table.

Hannah glanced at the intricate design, glad only she would notice the mistakes she'd made working long into the nights. "I couldn't ask everyone else to donate and not provide something myself." She shook her head at him. "You paid too much for it. I would've made you another one after we get married."

"I figured I was just contributing to my own salary. Besides, I recognized something in it." With his free hand, Gabe reached out to trace a repeating triangle of blue fabric in the multicolored quilt.

Hannah also touched the vibrant hue that matched the curtains in Gabe's apartment. Her finger slid over to the beige material right next to it. With a smile that she knew echoed the one in her eyes, she walked her fingers back to the blue.

Clasping Gabe's hand, she looked up at him. "Thank you for seeing me as more than I saw myself."

Gabe raised her hand to his lips and gently kissed the back of it. "Hannah." His voice was hoarse. "There's not enough fabric in the world to represent the color you bring into my life. I found and lost you in my past. And I will want for very little, as long as I have you in my present and future. That's the greatest thing I could ever have asked for."

* * * * *

Dear Reader,

Thanks so much for reading Hannah and Gabe's story! For them, and us, much is lost for want of asking. I found that pearl of wisdom on a coworker's daily calendar one year. It became my adage enough that our son-in-law used the philosophy to start a guitar program at the elementary school where he taught music. He was invited to present his project at the National Music Educator's conference, and while there, surprisingly gave his mother-in-law's adage credit for helping get the program launched.

Much is lost for want of asking. Sometimes the answer is no, and depending on the situation, that may be very hard to live with at that time. But sometimes the answer is yes, and such a yes that leads you to marvelous things you never even anticipated. Hannah wants to follow God's will for her life. Sometimes, it's hard to know what that will is. Sometimes I forget to ask. Sometimes when I do, I'm so busy looking down at my feet that I don't realize the amazing things that have been put together until I look back and say "Wow" at how God was laying things out all along.

I can't thank you enough for joining me on this journey. More Miller's Creek stories are coming. In the meantime, look me up at Jocelyn McClay on Facebook or connect with me at jocelynmcclay@gmail.com.

May God bless you and yours,
Jocelyn McClay

COMING NEXT MONTH FROM
Love Inspired

Available February 23, 2021

A SECRET AMISH CRUSH
Brides of Lost Creek • by Marta Perry
Running a small Amish coffee shop is all Lydia Stoltzfus needs to be satisfied with her life—until her next-door neighbor and childhood crush, Simon Fisher, returns home with his five-year-old daughter. Now even as she falls for the shy little girl, Lydia must resist her growing feelings for Simon…

AMISH BABY LESSONS
by Patrice Lewis
When Jane Troyer moves to a new Amish community to help in her aunt and uncle's store, she never expects to become a nanny. But suddenly Levy Struder needs help caring for his newborn niece, and Jane's wonderful with babies. Might their temporary arrangement turn into forever?

HERS FOR THE SUMMER
Wyoming Sweethearts • by Jill Kemerer
Eden Page reluctantly agrees to babysit Ryder Fanning's five-year-old identical twin daughters—but only for the summer. After that, she's taking charge of her own life. But this cowboy who's determined never to marry again could give her everything she wants…including the family and ranch she loves.

HIDING IN ALASKA
Home to Owl Creek • by Belle Calhoune
Forced to reinvent herself in witness protection, Isabelle Sanchez begins working for an Alaskan chocolate company. Though she's drawn to her new boss and heir to the chocolate empire, Connor North, she may never be able to tell him the truth. Can they find love despite her secrets?

A BROTHER'S PROMISE
Bliss, Texas • by Mindy Obenhaus
After his sister's death, rancher Mick Ashford will do anything to ensure his orphaned niece feels at home. And accepting guidance from Christa Slocum, who understands little Sadie's pain, is his first step. But when Sadie's paternal grandparents sue for custody, can they keep their makeshift family together?

A TEXAS BOND
Hill Country Cowboys • by Shannon Taylor Vannatter
When Ross Lyles discovers his younger brother has twins he never told the family about, Ross is determined to get to know his niece and nephew. But when he shows up at their aunt's ranch, Stacia Keyes is worried he'll try to take the children…and lassoing her trust is harder than he ever imagined.

LOOK FOR THESE AND OTHER LOVE INSPIRED BOOKS WHEREVER BOOKS ARE SOLD, INCLUDING MOST BOOKSTORES, SUPERMARKETS, DISCOUNT STORES AND DRUGSTORES.

LICNM0221

Get 4 FREE REWARDS!

We'll send you 2 FREE Books plus 2 FREE Mystery Gifts.

Love Inspired books feature uplifting stories where faith helps guide you through life's challenges and discover the promise of a new beginning.

FREE Value Over **$20**

"You want me to say you were right about Aunt Bess
and the matchmaking, don't you? Okay, you were right,"
Simon said.

"I thought you'd come to see it my way," Lydia said
lightly. "It didn't take your aunt long to get started, did
it?"

His only answer was a growled one. "You wouldn't
understand."

"Look, I do see what the problem is," she said. "You
don't want people to start thinking that you're tied up
with me when you have someone else in mind."

"I don't have anyone in mind." Simon sounded as if
he'd reached the end of his limited patience. "I'm not
going to marry again—not you, not anyone. I found love
once, and I don't suppose anyone has a second chance at
a love like that."

His bleak expression wrenched her heart, and she couldn't find any response.

He frowned, staring at the table as if he were thinking of something. "What do you suppose would happen if I hinted to Aunt Bess that I was thinking that way, but that I really needed to get to know you without scaring you off?"

"I don't know. She might be even worse. Still, I guess you could try it."

"Not just me," he said. "You'd have to at least act as if you were willing to be friends."

Somehow she had the feeling that she'd end up regretting this. But on the other hand, he could hardly discourage her from trying to help Becky in that case.

"Just one thing. If we're supposed to be becoming friends, then you won't be angry if I take an interest in Becky now, will you?"

He nodded. "All right. But…" He seemed to grow more serious. "If this makes you uncomfortable for any reason, we stop."

She tried to chase away the little voice in her mind that said she'd get hurt if she got too close to him. "No problem," she said firmly, and slammed the door on her doubts.

Don't miss
A Secret Amish Crush
by Marta Perry, available wherever
Love Inspired books and ebooks are sold.

LoveInspired.com

HARLEQUIN

If you enjoy the happily-ever-afters of Love Inspired books, try another great series from Harlequin!

With a wide range of romance series that each offer new books every month, you are sure to find the satisfying escape you deserve.

PASSION
Harlequin DARE
Harlequin Desire
Harlequin Presents

HOPE & INSPIRATION
Love Inspired
Harlequin Heartwarming

SUSPENSE
Harlequin Intrigue
Harlequin Romantic Suspense
Love Inspired Suspense

LIFE & LOVE
Harlequin Special Edition
Harlequin Medical Romance
Harlequin Romance

HISTORICAL
Harlequin Historical

**FIND YOUR FAVORITE SERIES IN STORE OR ONLINE,
OR SUBSCRIBE TO THE READER SERVICE!**

LIIBC2021

LOVE INSPIRED
INSPIRATIONAL ROMANCE

Choosing between her community…

and the man she still loves.

Five years ago, Hannah Lapp walked away from Gabe Bartel, crushing their dreams of a future together. She couldn't break her parents' hearts by marrying a Mennonite man and leaving the Amish community. Now Gabe is back as her town's new EMT. And Hannah's heart is on the line all over again, because this time she can't imagine letting him go…

CATEGORY: **HOPE & INSPIRATION**

$5.99 U.S./$6.99 CAN.

ISBN-13: 978-1-335-48866-4

50599

9 781335 488664

EAN

Uplifting stories of faith, forgiveness and hope.

HARLEQUIN
LOVE INSPIRED
harlequin.com